A Dyed B Dead Body

A Bekki the Beautician Cozy Mystery

Cindy Bell

Copyright © 2013 Cindy Bell

All rights reserved.

All rights reserved. No part of this publication may be reproduced or transmitted in any form or by any means, electronic or mechanical, including photocopy, recording, or any information storage or retrieval system, without permission in writing from the publisher.

This is a work of fiction. The characters, incidents and locations portrayed in this book and the names herein are fictitious. Any similarity to or identification with the locations, names, characters or history of any person, product or entity is entirely coincidental and unintentional.

All trademarks and brands referred to in this book are for illustrative purposes only, are the property of their respective owners and not affiliated with this publication in any way. Any trademarks are being used without permission, and the publication of the trademark is not authorized by, associated with or sponsored by the trademark owner.

ISBN-13: 978-1493630998

ISBN-10: 1493630997

More Cozy Mysteries by Cindy Bell

Heavenly Highland Inn Cozy Mystery Series

Murdering the Roses

Dead in the Daisies

Bekki the Beautician Cozy Mystery Series

Hairspray and Homicide

Mascara and Murder

Pageant and Poison

Conditioner and a Corpse

Table of Contents

Chapter One 1

Chapter Two 19

Chapter Three 50

Chapter Four 87

Chapter Five 109

Chapter One

It looked like the stars were winking. The entire sky full of them. As if they were offering to keep her secret. She knew that it was just clouds filtering across them, ushered by a light wind, but she preferred to think they were winking just the same. The bed of the truck was bumpy against the thin long sleeved blouse she wore. Her comfortable jeans were bent at the knees as she pushed her feet down. It was a cool autumn evening and she could hear what leaves remained fluttering on their branches. There were a few crickets, buzzing mosquitoes, and various other natural sounds, but no rush of traffic, no blaring of horns. It still amazed her, how quiet Harroway could be. Her hometown was a place she had never appreciated enough when she was a teenager, a place she couldn't wait to get away from. But now that she was back, she couldn't imagine a better place to be. Of course, that might be because of the company.

"Are you cold," he whispered from where he lay beside her. Nick Malonie, her high school summer fling, was laying next to her beneath the stars, just as they had so long ago. When she tipped her head to the side to look at him, her clear blue eyes meeting his dark green gaze, she took a sharp breath. For an instant she wondered if it was a dream. Their lips dangerously close, their breath mingled in the chill of the evening.

"Yes," she heard herself lie. As she hoped he would, he slid his arm around her and pulled her body close to his. The warmth of his presence was something she never thought she'd experience again. She smiled a little, and turned her head away to hide it.

"Better?" he murmured, a few strands of his light brown hair fluttering across his forehead.

"Mmm," she replied without looking back at him. She didn't want him to notice the blush rising along her olive skin. It was bad enough to wonder if he could hear the pounding of her heart. She felt like a teenager again, nervously anticipating a first kiss. Since she had been back in town she could not deny the draw she felt to Nick, but after experiencing a recent heartbreak, she found it difficult to believe that anything about love was real. She had caught her boyfriend of two years cheating on her, that was what had sent her running back to Harroway, and her mother's beauty salon. And to Nick.

"So beautiful," he sighed as he looked back up at the sky. "Do you remember staying out here until dawn?"

"I remember," she replied softly, keeping her eyes on the stars above her. They both fell silent for a long moment as he had broached a subject they had been avoiding. Once their passion had been wild, of course they had been kids, but it had felt like forever in the moment. Then all of a sudden Nick had disappeared for two months.

"And here we are again," Nick muttered. She felt him shift beside her so that he was leaning up on his elbow and looking down at her. He trailed a few strands of her wavy dark hair away from her face so that he could look into her eyes more easily.

"Sort of," she smiled and studied his eyes.

"What do you mean sort of?" he asked, not showing any sign that he would look away.

"Well, back then we were on a blanket in the grass, because you weren't allowed to take the truck out after dark," she smiled affectionately as she recalled how strict his father had been with him. Maybe that was what had driven him into law enforcement, the amount of rules he had to follow as a youth. Her own parents had been more flexible, and trusting of their daughter.

"Right," he lowered his voice to a barely audible whisper, and casually drew his lips closer to hers as he did. "And as I recall, you weren't allowed to sneak boys in through your bedroom window, Rebekah."

When he spoke her name it sent a shiver along her spine. Everyone in the world called her Bekki, even her parents. Her mother had admitted once that if she could have gotten away with naming her Bekki she would have, but her own mother had insisted on something more traditional. Only one person ever used her full name aside from teachers and business contacts.

"True," she agreed breathlessly, noting the heat growing in his eyes.

"So, is that rule still in place?" he arched a brow mischievously. It was a good question, considering that Bekki was now living in a home that her parents had bought.

"It didn't matter then and it doesn't now," she found herself grinning.

"So here we are, again," he reiterated and the flash in his eyes was as bright as the starlight shimmering above them.

"Well Nick, if I didn't know you were a fine upstanding police officer, I would think you were trying to seduce me," she smirked.

"I'm off duty," he explained and lowered his lips to the curve of her neck. He nuzzled them there for a moment, and she shuddered in reaction. The tension had grown between them, and though they hadn't officially started anything up, it was clear they both wanted to.

Still, it made Bekki a little nervous. When his lips trailed their way up along the side of her neck, she turned her head, intent on connecting them with her own. He lifted his chin, and in a split second the memories of their youth became the reality of their present day. The sensual caress was more potent than any embrace that Bekki could recall. Not that she could recall much of anything at that moment.

Her fingertips wandered up along the back of

his neck to toy lightly with the hair against his collar. He smiled through the kiss, and deepened it.

"Excuse me," they both jumped as they heard a voice, followed by the rap of a flashlight against the side of the bed of the truck. "Are you aware that you're trespassing?" the man standing beside the truck demanded. He flicked on the flashlight in his hand and shone it in their faces. Nick glared in the direction of the flashlight as Bekki laughed and buried her head in Nick's shoulder.

"Oh Detective Malonie, I'm sorry," the younger officer stammered. He was a rookie. "I didn't know it was you, I just saw the truck, and I figured it was a couple of kids out after curfew, uh," he smiled faintly. "Hi Bekki."

"Hi Morris," she mumbled and tried not to laugh again.

"Were you planning on arresting me Morris?" Nick asked with a furrowed brow.

"Of course not, no," Morris shook his head quickly.

"Then get out of here," Nick demanded with a

touch of his temper showing.

"Right, sorry, so sorry," Morris nearly tripped over his feet in an attempt to get back to his patrol car.

"You haven't given him a gun yet, have you?" Bekki asked nervously.

"No," Nick sighed and slumped back against the bed of the truck. "Now where were we," he murmured and leaned forward, ready to kiss her again.

"You were about to drive me home," she smiled at him and sat up. He stared after her with wide eyes.

"But it's still early," he pointed out as he sat up beside her.

"Nick, it's after curfew," she laughed and climbed out of the bed of the truck. He watched her for a long moment, and she knew that he could see right through her. The truth was she was relieved that Morris had shown up when he did. She wasn't sure she could control herself around Nick. She wasn't sure she was ready to risk getting hurt again, just yet.

"All right," he sighed as he jumped down from the truck. "I'll take you home," he kissed her cheek softly. "If you promise to go to dinner with me."

"Dinner?" she smiled a little.

"A real date," he clarified and held her gaze.

"Oh," she hesitated for a split second and then nodded. "Of course, I'd love to."

"All right," he smiled and held open the door of the truck for her. As Bekki climbed into the truck she smiled to herself. If there was ever a person she wanted a second chance with, it was Nick. She just wasn't sure if she was quite ready for it.

***

The next day Bekki slipped away from the salon at lunch to visit the new bakery in town. It was only a few stores down, but she walked around the block before heading towards it. She had a very special order to make, and she was trying to keep it a secret. When she had moved back into town she had been reunited with her best childhood friend Sammy, who worked at the salon with Bekki's mother. Tomorrow was

Sammy's birthday, and Bekki wanted to surprise her with a small party and cake. The bakery was a recent addition to the quaint little town square. It used to be a flower shop, but had been purchased by a woman named Lydia Michaels who had recently moved into town from Chicago. Although the townspeople of Harroway didn't always react warmly to strangers, Lydia fitted in just fine. She was very friendly and always willing to take custom orders. When Bekki stepped inside the bakery she found Lydia decorating some cupcakes.

"Hi Lydia," Bekki said cheerfully as she walked up to the counter.

"Hi Bekki," Lydia smiled as she looked up at the woman. Lydia had dark red hair frosted lightly with gray that Bekki had taken the time to curl into a nice style. It looked very good on her, but then Lydia always looked very pristine. That was one thing that Bekki and Lydia had in common, Lydia liked the city style of fashion as much as Bekki did. On the first day Bekki had met her, Lydia remarked on the purse she was carrying, the newest one of the season. Bekki still indulged in keeping up with trends as, even though she had left the city life behind, she really enjoyed staying in fashion.

"Oh would you look at those earrings," Lydia gushed as Bekki leaned over the counter to look over the selection of cake styles available.

"Oh these?" Bekki arched a brow mischievously as if she hadn't purposefully swept her hair back away from them to show them off. They were silver spirals that spun endlessly with the slightest touch. Bekki thought they were a bit young for her, but she was entranced by the seemingly endless movement, so she had bought them anyway.

"So beautiful," Lydia sighed. "I'm sure I saw Angelina wearing those."

"Really?" Bekki gasped. "I must have missed that. Do you want a pair? I could order some for you. I'm friends with a woman who works on the jewelry line, and she can get me a discount."

"Thank you so much," Lydia replied. "But only if they come in gold, I'm allergic to all other metals," she tapped the small gold hoops she was wearing in her ears.

"I'll check," Bekki assured her. "I was

wondering if you could whip up a special birthday cake for me, for tomorrow," she said apologetically, "I know it's last minute."

"No problem," Lydia smiled. "What type of cake would you like?"

"I was thinking two layers, Black Forest. It's her favorite," she explained and smiled as she recalled when Sammy and her had devoured an entire cake by themselves. One thing was for sure neither of them had ever lacked an appetite.

"My specialty," Lydia grinned. "I'll have it ready for you by tonight if you'd like to pick it up."

"That would be perfect," Bekki nodded with a smile of relief. "But I am closing the salon tonight, so it will be after the shop closes. Maybe I could pick it up in the morning?"

"Don't worry about it," Lydia waved her hand dismissively. "I'm always here late after the store closes. I'll just leave the back door open for you, and you come on in when you're done at the salon. Maybe we can have a coffee, hmm?"

"Sounds lovely," Bekki agreed. "Thanks again Lydia."

"Anytime," the warmth in her smile really made it seem as if she was pleased to be part of the party planning. "See you tonight."

"Bye," Bekki called as she hurried back out of the shop. She needed to get back to the salon before Sammy got suspicious.

As she walked in the direction of the salon she smiled to herself. She was sure her friend had no idea what she was planning, and that was just how she was going to keep it. After years of barely keeping in touch, she knew she had some birthdays to make up for.

***

As soon as Bekki stepped into the salon she was met with Sammy's scathing glare.

"Where have you been?" Sammy demanded to know. She was obviously frazzled, and Bekki could see why. There were several women in the waiting room. It wasn't usually a busy day but apparently there was a new bachelor in town and several of the women were vying for his attention.

"I'm sorry, I just needed to run an errand," Bekki frowned as her friend scowled in her direction. The salon was a place that Bekki had grown up in. She had spent many afternoons playing at the reception desk or sweeping up hair, while her mother, who was the owner of the salon, took care of customers. As a result, in many ways the whole town had been part of Bekki's childhood. There were very few townspeople that she didn't know.

"I'll take whoever is next," Bekki announced, hoping to make up for dropping the ball. As she ushered a woman to one of the open chairs, she overheard a couple of the other women gossiping.

"Oh yes, I was over there last week," Ethel nodded with a smirk. "Very hoity toity with her fancy cupcakes."

"Not at all," Sue insisted across from them. "She's a lovely woman, and her baked goods are delicious. I mean, have you had her cookies?"

"Well yes," Ethel admitted and licked her lips lightly. "They were quite tasty. But who needs all that fancy decoration?"

"Young people," Sue replied sternly. "Right, Bekki? You kids just can't have a cookie without a little design on it now, right?"

Bekki laughed out loud at being called a kid and shook her head as she combed through the fine blonde hair of the woman in her chair.

"Well, it never hurts to make things look pretty ladies, now does it?" she told them with a sweet smile and they all laughed.

"That's true, we could all use a little decoration," Ethel laughed loudly and soon the entire salon was buzzing with a jovial energy. After a few customers, the salon began to empty out a bit.

"Sammy, do you need a break?" Bekki offered as she glanced over at her friend.

"Oh no it's all right, I'm off tomorrow," she shrugged casually but from the way she said tomorrow it was obvious that she expected Bekki to know why. Bekki had not made any mention of her birthday, as if she had forgotten completely.

"Oh that's true," Bekki nodded a little. "I'll miss you," she sighed dramatically.

"Sure," Sammy laughed and shook her head.

"Oh Ethel, did you hear about Morris' first act as a rookie officer last night?" she smirked and her eyes took on a devilish gleam.

"Sammy!" Bekki groaned.

"Oh yes I heard all about it," Ethel laughed loudly as Bekki rinsed the soap from her hair. "Something about a couple of lovers curled up in the starlight, he scared the passion right out of them."

Bekki blushed deeply and glared in Sammy's direction.

"Oh so you didn't hear who it was?" Sammy teased.

"Well no, do you know?" Ethel asked intrigued.

"I heard about it," Sue sang out from the waiting area. She would often stick around even after her hair was done just to spend time with her friends. "Now don't you blush Bekki, you weren't doing anything wrong. That rascal Nick should know the law, after all."

"Is that so?" Nick asked as he stepped into the salon and flashed Sue a disarming grin. "Well, I'll have you know, I was off duty."

"Hmph," Ethel called out as she moved under one of the dryers. "You might be off duty, but there's still a curfew in this town!"

"For the teenagers," Bekki reminded Ethel.

"Well," Ethel smirked in a sassy way. "If you two are going to go about behaving like teenagers, then you should obey the curfew too."

Nick laughed out loud and shook his head as Bekki rolled her eyes to the ceiling. It was easy to think of herself as a teenager again when she was surrounded by the women who had watched her grow up.

"Hi Nick," she said sweetly, to change the subject. "Is this an official visit?"

"No, no," Nick shook his head slightly and met Bekki's gaze over the top of her customer's head. He was still regretting their night getting cut short. "I'm here to invite you to dinner."

"How delightful," Bekki replied with a smile as if she had not texted him a few minutes before and asked him to do just that. "Well, I'd be honored. When?"

"Tomorrow night," Nick said swiftly. "If you're available."

Sammy dropped her scissors on the counter of her station. Bekki ignored the clatter and pretended to be thinking about it.

"Yes I do believe I'm free. Six sound okay?" she inquired.

"Perfect," he replied. He nodded his head to Sammy. "Good to see you Sammy."

"You too," Sammy replied dryly and did not even attempt to hide her look of contempt. She was not pleased that her best friend had just made plans on her birthday.

"All right then, I'll see you tomorrow night," Nick said as he glanced at his watch. "Better get back. I left Morris in charge of the cross walk."

"Oh dear, last time I had a bag of groceries he nearly picked me up and carried me," Sue giggled.

"He's very enthusiastic," Nick agreed and winked at Sue.

"Afternoon ladies," he nodded to them all as he stepped out of the salon.

17

"Oh isn't he delicious," Ethel sighed dreamily. Sammy pushed the dryer down over her head and flipped it on.

"Sure he's great," she muttered.

After Ethel was finished, Bekki could tell that Sammy was getting more irritated by the moment.

"You have the day off tomorrow, why not head home early?" Bekki suggested. She wanted to make sure that Sammy wasn't around when she picked up the cake. "I can close up."

"Perfect," Sammy sighed and gathered her things. She paused by the front door of the salon and glanced back at Bekki.

"So I guess I'll see you on Wednesday," she said with a shrug.

"Sure," Bekki nodded barely glancing up from the papers on her desk. "Night!"

"Night," Sammy frowned and stepped out of the salon. As Bekki looked up and watched her friend walk sullenly away, she wondered if she should let her in on the truth. But she didn't want to tip her off to the party she was planning.

Chapter Two

After closing up the shop for the night Bekki made sure the coast was clear. With no sign of Sammy anywhere she walked directly over to the bakery. The front blinds were down, and she knew the door would be locked. She walked around the side of the building towards the rear of the shop. When she reached the back door she found it unlocked as expected. She opened the door and stepped inside.

"Lydia?" she called out as the inside of the bakery was dark. She wondered if she might have gone home already and forgotten to lock up. She flipped the switch on and flooded the kitchen with light. There were still some ingredients sitting out that Bekki was sure Lydia would have put away before going home for the night. She began to feel a little uneasy as she walked towards the front of the shop.

"Lydia?" she called out again, hopefully. She froze as she stood behind the counter of the bakery. Before her was a silhouette. A figure was hanging from a noose tied to a rafter in the ceiling. "Lydia?" Bekki whispered in horror as she flipped on the light. Lydia's body was revealed instantly, dangling limply from the noose.

"No!" Bekki shouted and ran forward to grab the woman's legs. She nearly tripped over a chair that had been kicked over beneath the woman. "Lydia," she gasped out, clinging to the woman's legs and trying to push her upward just in case she might still be breathing. But she knew from her ice cold legs, she knew that Lydia was already dead. Bekki could not hold back her tears as she fumbled in her pocket for her phone and dialed the police. As soon as they were on the way she dialed Nick's personal cell.

"Nick," she sobbed into the phone. "Nick, get to the bakery fast."

Within minutes officers had arrived along with paramedics. Only then did Bekki let go of Lydia. The paramedics shook their heads sadly as there was no sign of life in the woman.

Bekki backed away from Lydia's body. Despite the fact that she was horrified by what had happened, Bekki's natural attention to detail had her focus in on a few things. On the floor not far from Lydia was what appeared to be a suicide note. It was written on a piece of dark blue paper, which seemed odd in itself. But its message was even stranger. It was a simple apology and goodbye. No real explanation for the action that Lydia had taken. It struck Bekki as odd that the note would be on the floor, not on a counter, or a table. If someone took the care to write a note, would they then toss it on the floor? She crouched down to take a closer look at it, and something else caught her eye.

"Don't touch it," Nick said sharply from the doorway of the bakery.

"I'm not," Bekki sniffled. She was looking past the note at the silver glint that had caught her eye. It was the back of an earring, easy to lose, impossible to find.

"Are you okay?" Nick asked breathlessly as he guided her up from the floor and pulled her into his arms.

"Nick, this can't be what it looks like," Bekki insisted quickly as the oddities of the situation began to add up in her mind. "There's no way Lydia killed herself. I just talked to her this afternoon, I just ordered Sammy's cake, I..."

"Shh," he murmured soothingly as he stroked his fingers down through her raven locks. "It's never easy when someone does something like this. We always think we know people, but we don't know everything."

"I'm telling you Nick," Bekki's voice grew a bit louder. "I just saw her, there is no way she was suicidal. And if she was, why would she have turned all the lights out? Why would she toss the note on the floor?" Bekki demanded.

Nick sighed as he studied her, attempting to be patient.

"You can't expect someone who is intent on taking their own life to act rationally, Bekki. This is pretty cut and dry. There's a note, for God's sake. I mean do you really think someone hoisted her up there?" he said a bit more crassly than he intended. "You have to listen to the evidence that is in front of you," he reminded her. He knew that Bekki liked to play detective. Truth be told she was good at it. "I know that Lydia was your friend," he added in a gentler tone. "It never makes sense when someone we care about chooses to end their life. But this one you're just going to have to accept Bekki."

Bekki blushed as all of the other officers were looking in their direction. She felt as if Nick was trying to put her in her place in front of his colleagues.

"No, I don't have to just accept that someone who was laughing and smiling with me a few hours ago decided it was time to end it all," Bekki replied in a subtle growl.

"Listen, you should go," he said sternly, his eyes growing darker with his frustration. "We're going to have to take her down, and I think it's best if you don't see that."

"Well if you think it's best," Bekki retorted, wondering why he didn't think it was best to listen to her suspicions. To her it was clear that something was not right. But Nick only nodded, holding her gaze with his own as he did. She pulled away from him and he sighed as he watched her storm off through the back door.

***

As Bekki made her way around the corner of the bakery she nearly collided with Sammy.

"Bekki, I heard the sirens, what's going on?" she asked with concern. "Did something happen?"

When Bekki stepped under a street lamp Sammy could see her cheeks were covered with tears.

"Oh no, are you okay?" Sammy gasped and pulled her into a gentle hug.

"It's Lydia," Bekki managed to get out. "It's Lydia."

"What's wrong? Did she get hurt?" Sammy frowned and pulled away from Bekki slightly to glance in the direction of the stretcher that the paramedics were wheeling slowly into the bakery. It was clear that they were not in a rush.

"She's dead," Bekki revealed and wiped furiously at her cheeks. "I stopped over to pick up your cake and..."

"Wait, what do you mean she's dead?" Sammy winced and tears began to fill her eyes. "Are you sure?"

"Yes," Bekki sniffled and tried to calm herself down. "I walked in the back door, she left it open for me, so I could get the cake." She held her breath for a moment before admitting, "they think it was suicide." She glowered in the direction of a few of the officers who stepped outside of the bakery.

"Was it?" Sammy asked in a hushed voice.

"I don't know," Bekki admitted and shook her head. "But it doesn't seem right. I was just there this afternoon, and she was fine. I ordered the cake…"

"The cake," Sammy interrupted. "You mean for my birthday?" Her eyes widening.

Bekki nodded, fresh tears gathering. "I wanted it to be a surprise, I'm sorry Sammy."

"No don't be sorry," Sammy hugged her. "It's just sad to think that one of the last things she was making was my cake. What if something about it made her sad enough to do this?"

Sammy's words made Bekki's heart slow down. She remembered Lydia's warm smile as she promised to leave the back door open for her. Her stomach lurched. What if she had arrived there just a little earlier? What if she hadn't waited so long to pick up the cake? Could she have saved Lydia?

"This is all just so horrible," Sammy sighed as she watched the stretcher get wheeled back out, this time with Lydia's body concealed in a dark bag.

"I just don't see how a person could go from being so happy, to wanting to die, in one afternoon," Bekki said quietly as her nerves finally began to settle. She caught sight of Nick as he paused in the doorway of the bakery. He was looking over something he had written in his notes. As eager as she had been to see him again, now the sight of him only infuriated her. Despite the fact that she was certain things were not as they seemed, he had not been willing to listen.

"We were going to have a party," Bekki heard herself saying before she even realized she was speaking, "for you."

Sammy squeezed Bekki's hand gently. "Don't worry about that Bekki, come on, let me take you home. You need to rest."

Bekki closed her eyes briefly, but all she saw was poor Lydia hanging from the rafter. After Sammy dropped her off at home Bekki lay on her bed with her eyes half open. The flickering shadows in her room kept reminding her of the things she had noticed at the bakery. The note on the floor, which held no personal information, and the back of a silver earring. This stuck in her mind for a long moment.

"Wait a minute," she murmured to herself. "That couldn't have belonged to Lydia, she only wore gold," her eyes widened as she realized this. She tried to sleep, but her mind was buzzing with the possibilities of just what might have really happened to Lydia.

**

The town awoke to the shock of the news of Lydia's apparent suicide. It was all anyone was thinking or talking about. Bekki cringed as she overheard some people talking about the horrible nature of suicide as she walked past them on the sidewalk towards the salon. She wanted to turn around and insist that this might not have been suicide after all, but she knew that would only alert people to her suspicions. So far all she had to base them on was a hunch. When she arrived at the salon she was surprised to find Sammy there.

"Happy birthday," Bekki said with a sad smile as she hugged her friend.

"I've postponed my birthday," Sammy said firmly. "Once everyone has a chance to say goodbye, we'll have dinner or something. It's just too sad to be happy about anything right now."

"I can understand that," Bekki nodded as she glanced through the front window of the salon at the people who had gathered outside of the bakery, some out of curiosity, some out of grief. "But you're still not going to work on your birthday. Home with you young lady," she demanded.

"I thought after last night that you might need the day off," Sammy explained with a light frown. "That must have been such a tragic thing to see."

"It was," Bekki agreed, her eyes growing distant as she recalled the scene. "But I'd rather be here, than at home obsessing about it. Working will take my mind off things," she managed a stern smile.

"All right," Sammy said reluctantly. "If you're sure?" she questioned one last time.

"I'm positive," Bekki insisted and hugged her friend again. "And even if it is a sad day, I am still going to wish you happy birthday."

"Thank you," Sammy smiled into her shoulder and gave her a squeeze. "Call me if you need anything, okay?" She met her eyes to be sure that she would.

"I will," Bekki promised as she sat down behind the reception desk. After Sammy left she spent most of her morning fielding calls from clients who were canceling their appointments. The town had come to a standstill as people tried to figure out how someone as cheerful and loving as Lydia had chosen to hang herself. Once the flurry of calls died down and Bekki was preparing to make a list of her suspicions, the door to the salon swung open. She glanced up and was surprised to find a woman about her age who was dressed in the finest and latest fashion. Bekki stood up from her chair as the woman walked further into the salon. Her delicate nose scrunched up at the sight of the simple place, and she cleared her throat.

"Well, I guess this will have to do," she mumbled to herself. Her glossy blonde hair was pulled back into a tight bun, and her eyes were hidden by a pair of dark sunglasses. She looked as if she belonged in a high end salon, certainly not Bekki's.

"Can I help you with something?" Bekki asked with a friendly smile.

"I just need a touch up on my roots, and maybe a bit of a style," the woman smiled in return, but there was more loftiness than friendliness in the expression. "Do you think you could do that?"

"I'm sure I can," Bekki replied, gritting her teeth. She never liked the prissy attitude of some of the wealthier women she had met in the city. This woman had plenty of attitude.

"Have a seat, and I'll be right with you," Bekki gestured to one of the open chairs. The woman walked over to it, her nose still scrunched. She pulled a tissue out of her pocket and wiped off the seat of the chair before sitting down. Then she tossed the tissue in a nearby waste basket. Bekki grabbed a new customer form and walked up beside her.

"Are you visiting?" she asked as she jotted down the woman's requests.

"Yes, just for a day or so," the woman

explained.

"My name is Bekki, welcome to Harroway," she managed to retain her friendly tone. She was not going to tarnish the town's good reputation over one woman's disrespectful behavior.

"I'm Julie," the woman replied sounding a little impatient. "Will this take long? I was hoping to get some lunch and do a little shopping this afternoon."

"Shopping? Here?" Bekki asked with surprise as she eased the woman's sunglasses off to reveal her pale green eyes. She walked behind her and began releasing the pins that held up her bun. "Don't worry it won't take long."

"Yes, there's a fabulous antique store I have been dying to visit," she exclaimed as if it was the most delightful excursion she could imagine. Bekki nodded in quiet agreement but she could not think of what antique store she might be talking about. As the woman's hair tumbled down to the base of her neck, Bekki reached forward and swept it back away from her ears. As she did her finger caught lightly on one of the woman's simple stud earrings. She noticed that the earring was silver, but the backing on it was a very different style. She glanced at the woman's other ear and found that the back of it matched its earring perfectly.

"Calm down," she told herself. Plenty of people lose those little backs to earrings, and replace them with others. But her mind was reeling at the sight. What were the chances of it being a coincidence? The woman prattled on about her shopping intentions.

"I am looking for small town memorabilia as I want to do a bit of a diner themed kitchen, you know, just for fun," she laughed. Her laughter was not real. It was the light and airy kind that Bekki always imagined women like her practiced in front of the mirror before they left the house each day.

"Well, you've come to the right place for that," Bekki said as pleasantly as she could. As she took the woman through the stages of touching up her roots, she tried to ask questions to put her mind at ease.

"Do you have a friend or family member who told you about Harroway?" she asked casually.

"No, I just happened upon it, lucky me," Julie

replied with a sly smile.

"Do you live far from here?" Bekki inquired, her words nothing more than the friendly banter of a hair stylist.

"I'm from Chicago, actually," Julie answered proudly. "But I'm a bit of a wanderer."

The name of the city burned into Bekki's mind. It was the same city that Lydia was from. Sure, there were plenty of people in Chicago, but what were the chances of two of them ending up in Harroway?

"I've heard Chicago is an amazing city," Bekki smiled. "I'll let this set for a few minutes. Would you like some tea, some water?" she suggested.

"No I'm fine thank you," Julie replied and settled back in her chair. Bekki's mind was filled with pieces of information that did not fit together. She could not comprehend what Lydia and Julie would have to do with each other, and yet she couldn't shake the certainty that there was a connection. When she returned to style Julie's hair she decided to ask a few bolder questions.

"Did you just get into town today?" she asked.

Maybe, if Julie had been there the day before, she had visited the bakery, and that would explain how her earring back might have ended up on the floor.

"Just this morning," Julie nodded and watched Bekki like a hawk as she arranged and styled her hair.

"Will you be staying long?" Bekki wondered as she gave the woman's hair a final fluff.

"Well, with such an amazing stylist as yourself, I might have to," Julie cooed as she smiled at herself in the mirror. Bekki tried not to let the compliment make her like the woman more but she couldn't help it. It meant a lot coming from someone as refined and obviously well off as her.

"Thank you," Bekki said genuinely. "I'm glad you like it."

"Now I can shop in style," the woman sighed with relief and followed Bekki over to the front desk. She handed her a card to pay with. Bekki held the card in her hand long enough to get a clear view of the woman's full name, then she ran it through.

"Well, I hope you enjoy your time here," Bekki said as she plastered on her brightest smile. "Everyone is very close here."

"Good to know," the woman said with an arched brow and then headed for the door. As soon as she was gone, Bekki grabbed a notepad and scribbled down her full name, Julie Ann Brentwood

"Julie Ann…," she said aloud.

"Who's that?" Nick asked as he entered the salon.

"How do you always do that?" Bekki demanded with exasperation.

"Do what?" he frowned as he walked up to the desk.

"You sneak in places, you're like a ninja," she huffed and quickly tucked away the notepad.

He quirked a brow and leaned across the desk, meeting her eyes boldly. "I am a ninja," he stated flatly. "There you know my deepest, darkest secret."

Bekki couldn't help but smile a little. She was still annoyed with him over the night before, but there was something about Nick that never allowed her to stay angry with him for long.

"All right then Ninja Nick, what brings you here? Need that ego trimmed a bit?" her lips curved into a cheeky smile.

"Excuse me?" he blinked at her words and his mouth dropped open slightly. "My ego?"

"Oh yes grand detective," she bowed her head playfully and looked back up at him.

"I am a police detective," he pointed out, tapping the top of the desk lightly. "I actually have training, and experience, and..."

"A shiny little badge," she smirked and batted her eyes sweetly.

"You're pushing it you know," he heaved a sigh, but she could see the sparkle of amusement in his eyes.

"Okay, fine, you're the detective," she waved her hand in his direction. "But that means I get to be the ninja, you can't be both, and I'm the one with the black belt."

"Well, you can wear it when I take you out to dinner tonight," he shrugged. "I thought since we're postponing Sammy's birthday party, we could actually have dinner instead."

"Don't you have anything you need to do about Lydia?" she asked nervously.

"Bekki," he frowned, his playfulness abandoned. "There's nothing to investigate. We've notified her family."

"Her family?" Bekki asked with surprise. She had never really thought about Lydia having much family.

"You see," he said with an air of authority. "You don't know everything about Lydia. She has a past, just like the rest of us, and it probably wasn't very pleasant."

Bekki wanted to argue the point but he was right. She didn't actually know that much about Lydia. "So dinner?" he prompted her.

"Sure," she nodded, feeling a little distracted.

"Meet me at Santini's around six?" he suggested. "I have some paperwork I have to file."

"I'll be there," Bekki assured him, her mind still on Lydia.

"So what was that name you were saying when I walked in?" he asked just as he was about to turn away.

"Oh, it's nothing," Bekki said swiftly. He narrowed his eyes slightly, as if she had given something away.

"Dinner," he reminded her and then leaned forward to kiss her gently on the cheek. Bekki savored the kiss and sighed as he pulled away.

"We could always just look at the stars instead," she smiled.

"Uh uh, proper date, remember?" He winked and walked out of the salon.

***

Bekki watched through the front window of the salon until she was certain that Nick was gone. Then she turned to the computer and opened up the internet. She did a web search for Julie Ann Brentwood. She didn't expect too much to come up, but right away the results flooded onto the screen. There were pictures of Julie in all kinds of fine gowns at some very exclusive events. She was nearly always on the arm of a man, Dan Brentwood. Until recently

Dan had been a billionaire bachelor. He was on all kinds of top twenty hottest lists. Not only was he very handsome, but he seemed to be involved in quite a few charities. He had made his riches himself, running his own business. A few months back he had made a big splash in the media by marrying Julie Ann. Julie seemed to enjoy his money and his connections. She was always offering a smile to the cameras and keeping a possessive hand on Dan's arm.

Bekki sat back in her chair as she studied the screen. None of this made anything clearer to her. Julie was apparently a very well off and practically famous person. But the pictures offered no explanation of what she might be doing in Harroway or what her connection with Lydia might be. Bekki did a few more searches on Julie but she could not find any information about her before she was with Dan. She couldn't even find the woman's maiden name, as if all evidence of it had been wiped away. With a sigh she closed the website and wondered if she had hit a dead end. How could she find out more information about Julie?

She began to wonder just what shops she

might be hitting during the afternoon. If she was staying in town, then there were a couple of little boutiques she could be visiting. If she was staying in town.

"That's it!" Bekki snapped her fingers and smiled as she seized on an idea. All she had to do was figure out where Julie was staying, then she could have a look inside her room. Of course it seemed much more simple in her mind than it actually would be, but that did not stop her. Bekki looked around the salon and found a scarf that someone had left behind. It looked elegant enough to belong to someone like Julie. She flipped the sign on the salon door to read "Closed" and locked the door behind her. As she headed down the sidewalk that wound through the majority of the town square, she kept turning over in her mind the clues that she had already found. She stopped in the first small boutique in a line of shops. When she stepped inside the owner was sorting through some necklaces. He glanced up and offered her a distracted smile.

"Bekki, what can I do for you?" he asked. It seemed just about everyone in town knew her name, although she didn't always remember their names.

"I'm looking for a woman who is visiting in town, her name is Julie," Bekki explained to the shop owner. "She left her scarf in the salon and I just want to figure out where she is staying so I can leave it for her."

"Oh yes, she was in here," the shop owner nodded with a grimace. "Tried on every pair of shoes in the place."

"Did she say where she was staying?" Bekki asked hopefully.

"Actually, she asked me to deliver her shoes to her motel," he chuckled and shrugged. "With the tip she left me I gladly agreed. She's staying at Harroway Harbor."

"Great, thanks!" Bekki smiled as she clutched the scarf. "I'm sure she'll be glad to get this back."

"No problem," the shop owner nodded and then lowered his voice. "Did you hear anything else about Lydia? Do you think she'll be buried here?"

"I don't know," Bekki frowned as she

considered this. "Nick did say her family was contacted, so I guess they will be making the arrangements."

"So sad," the shop owner sighed with a slow shake of his head. "I never would have thought Lydia would do something like that."

"Did you know her well?" Bekki asked curiously.

"Not as well as I thought," he frowned and stared hard at the counter top. "I just don't understand it. She never seemed anything but happy."

"I know," Bekki nodded in agreement. "She certainly didn't seem to be someone who was giving up on life."

He sighed, his shoulders slumping as a wry smile reached his lips. "Well, you know what they say, you never truly know everything about anyone."

"I guess so," Bekki gave the back of his hand a gentle pat. "Thanks for your help."

"You're welcome," he smiled as he turned back to the necklaces he was arranging. As Bekki stepped out of the shop it struck her that so many people seemed to be stunned by Lydia's suicide, and yet none of them questioned whether it was true. Just as Nick had pointed out, all of the evidence made it a clear suicide. But what about Lydia herself? Nothing about the woman Bekki had known pointed to her being depressed or upset about life. That had to count for something didn't it?

The Harroway Harbor was right at the edge of the town square. It was a small motel with only twelve rooms, but it did a decent enough business. Travelers would often stop over on their way to somewhere else. Family and friends of those who lived in town would stay there. It had a good reputation for being clean and friendly. But, it was certainly not a place that Bekki would expect a woman to stay who was as well off and used to the finer things of life as Julie seemed to be. On the way to the motel she stopped off at the salon and gathered up a few brochures. She couldn't exactly just walk into the motel with no purpose, she needed an excuse for being there. When she arrived at the motel she paused outside and considered what she was about to do. Nick had made it clear that he wanted her to stay out of it. She didn't think breaking and entering really counted as staying out of it.

She closed her eyes briefly and remembered the kiss they had shared in the bed of his truck. It had been one of the most memorable she had ever experienced. She knew there was so much more to explore between them. If she was caught committing a crime, would that be it for them? As much as she valued her chance to get to know Nick again, that did not stop her from wanting to find out the truth for Lydia. After all, no one else was looking for an explanation, and if Bekki let it go, whatever family Lydia had would spend the rest of their lives believing that their loved one had committed suicide. And a murderer would get away with a terrible crime.

More determined than ever, Bekki pulled open the door of the motel and stepped inside.

***

"Hi," Bekki smiled sweetly at the clerk behind the counter. He looked like he was barely out of his teens and his mind was on the computer game he was playing. "I run the beauty salon in town, and I was wondering if I could just drop a few brochures off, near the elevators and in the common areas. Would that be okay?"

"Sure," he shrugged, barely looking away from the screen.

"Thanks," Bekki hurried off before he could change his mind. Once she was in the hallway that led to some of the rooms, she realized she still had no idea what room the woman was staying in. The rooms had thick doors and no way to peer inside of them. None of them had a big sign outside declaring that a very wealthy woman was staying there. She was starting to lose confidence in her plan when she turned the corner in the hall. She noticed a cleaning cart outside one of the rooms. If anyone knew everything that happened in a motel, it was the maid. Just as she reached the cart, the maid stepped out of the room it was parked in front of and reached for a spray bottle on the top of the cart.

"Hello," Bekki smiled at the young woman. She recognized her from the salon, she was sure of it. "I'm just dropping off some brochures."

"Oh, okay," the woman smiled in return and snatched up a clean rag.

"Crazy everything that's been happening around here, huh?" Bekki asked casually as she lingered by the cart.

"Sure is," the woman agreed with a light shrug. Bekki winced inwardly as she realized the maid wasn't the talkative type. She was young, and seemed to be dedicated to her job, or perhaps she had just learned to stay out of the guests' business. Bekki lowered her voice a little, as if she was sharing a secret as she spoke.

"You know I had a customer today, I could have sworn that she was a celebrity or something. Have no idea what she's doing in Harroway," she said shifting gears into a more gossipy tone. Her clear blue eyes searched the woman's face for any sign of recognition. She didn't have to wait long.

"Oh, you mean the rich lady?" the young girl inquired. "She's staying here. In room nine. I just cleaned it," she grinned, but then her smile faded. "I don't know how it is that someone can have so much money and travel so lightly. I thought there would be lots of suitcases and dresses in the closet, but nothing," she raised her eyebrows with a surprise. "Just one little bag."

"Really?" Bekki said thoughtfully. "Well maybe she's roughing it," she laughed a little.

"Maybe," the woman grinned. "Anyway, I have to get back to work," she offered another polite smile to Bekki and then ducked back into the room she was cleaning. Bekki noticed the key ring hanging off the end of the cart. It appeared to contain the keys for each of the rooms, as each was labeled with a number. She waited until she heard the squeak of the spray bottle, then swiftly snatched the keys. She held them tightly to keep them from jingling as she walked down the hall to room nine. With a quick glance down the hallway she unlocked the door and stepped inside. She closed the door swiftly behind her. She knew that she wouldn't have much time to look. If the maid found the keys missing, she would be in serious trouble. What the maid had said was true. There was barely any luggage, or anything else for that matter. Nothing in the bathroom, nothing in the trash can, nothing at all to implicate Julie. Bekki was just about to give up when she noticed something on the desk. It was a dark blue notepad. The same color paper that was used for Lydia's suicide note.

"This is it!" Bekki squealed as she snatched up the notepad. She was certain that with this as proof, Nick would have to believe her. She tucked it behind her back under her blouse and hurried out of the room. She was just dropping the keys back onto the cart, when the maid stepped out of the room. She looked at Bekki strangely as if she wondered if she had stood there the entire time.

"Is everything okay?" she asked suspiciously.

"I'm sorry I was so rude earlier," Bekki said quickly, her heart pounding as she wondered if the maid had seen her with the keys. "I didn't even give you a brochure. Come in any time, I'll give you a free style with a cut or a manicure if you prefer, okay?"

The woman looked a little skeptical at first, but then the offer of a freebie coaxed a smile out of her.

"Great, thanks," she nodded and accepted the brochure. "I'll be in soon," she promised. Bekki left the motel as fast as she could, glancing in both directions to make sure that Julie was not on her way back. Now she was certain that the woman whose hair she had just touched up and styled was not just a very wealthy woman, but a cold blooded killer. She didn't want to chance a face to face encounter with Julie just yet. She needed to get Nick on her side first.

Chapter Three

When she returned to the salon she had hoped she would have time to call Nick, but she found a few customers waiting outside.

"Hi ladies," she managed to smile at them. As the gloom of the day had begun to wear off people wanted their curls freshened or their style primped for the funeral. Bekki knew what they really wanted to do was gossip about Lydia. She unlocked the door and allowed the customers in, her mind still spinning with the evidence she had found.

"I for one saw it coming," one of the women said to the other. "It was obvious. That bakery was never going to make it. It's clear she was having financial trouble."

Bekki rolled her eyes and ignored the rumor. She knew that Lydia's business had been doing well. Once she had each of the ladies settled in chairs, she slipped the notepad out of her blouse and into the top drawer of the reception desk. She hoped that Nick would still consider it usable evidence even if he wasn't able to lift prints off it. At least it would convince him that she was right, and maybe he would begin a real investigation.

She hurried the customers through their hairstyles. Luckily they were so busy talking that they didn't notice Bekki being a little less friendly than usual. Despite the fact that Bekki was rushing, when she glanced at the clock it was nearly time to close. She took payment from the women and thanked them, but refused to be drawn into a longer conversation. When they still lingered she cleared her throat.

"I'm sorry ladies, but I really need to be closing up," she attempted to explain.

"Oh, of course," one of the women said. "It's just feels so eerie walking past the bakery," she sighed.

"It is," Bekki nodded. "Maybe you could go around the other way."

'And miss out on all the drama?" the other woman gasped and winked lightly. "Now Bekki, we couldn't possibly do that."

Bekki smiled a little, but she didn't want to laugh at Lydia's fate. She didn't want to consider it nothing more than drama. She was a person who had been living the life she wanted, and for some reason, Julie Brentwood had taken that opportunity from her. Bekki was going to find out why.

After she closed up for the night she noticed Morris escorting a man into the bakery. She only caught a glimpse of his face and his expensive suit, but it was enough for her to recognize him. It was Dan Brentwood, Julie's husband! What was he doing going into the bakery? She sneaked up closer to the bakery in time to hear their conversation.

"I'm very sorry for your loss," Morris said politely. "Your mother had become a part of our little town, and we're here to help you, with whatever you may need."

"Thank you," Dan replied, his voice trembling as he spoke. Bekki gasped as she heard Morris declare that Dan was Lydia's son. They didn't share a last name, but she was sure there were any number of explanations for that. If Lydia wanted a private life in contrast to her son's very public one, then she might have been using her maiden name. She stepped closer to the bakery and peered through the front window as Morris walked Dan inside. She watched as Dan paused in front of the counter. All evidence of the suicide had been removed, but Dan seemed to instinctively know the last spot where his mother had been.

"How could this happen?" she heard him sob as he leaned on the counter for support. "Why didn't she just call me?"

"I'm so sorry sir," Morris said nervously, overwhelmed and uncertain as to how to comfort the man. Bekki drew back into the shadows when Dan turned to look out the front window of the bakery.

"If only I had known," he said sadly, staring through the thick glass.

***

On the way to her house on Rose Hill Drive, she called Nick. After several rings she heard his voicemail message.

"Nick, it's Bekki. Call me please," she said swiftly. When she drove past Nick's house she noticed that his car was not in the drive. Bekki's house was dark when she entered it. The shadowy environment gave her a sudden flashback to walking into the back of the bakery. She tried to ignore the unease she felt in the pit of her stomach and flipped the hall light on. As she walked further into the house she dialed Nick's number again. Once again she got his voicemail. She was getting frustrated. She wanted to prove to him that there was a reason to suspect that Lydia had been murdered. She couldn't do that if he wouldn't answer her calls.

"Nick," she pleaded. "It's really important, please, I need to talk to you. I've got real evidence that Lydia didn't kill herself. It wasn't a suicide Nick, I swear."

She wondered where he could be, what he could be doing that he wasn't answering the phone. Then all at once she remembered. She was supposed to meet Nick for dinner. She glanced down at her watch to see that it was well after seven. The numbers on her watch suddenly blurred as a sharp pain flooded her head from the base of her skull. She was aware that something had struck her very hard from behind, and then her body collapsed to the floor as the pain overtook her. Through barely parted lashes she caught sight of a hand reaching down for the notepad that had landed on the floor beside her, then she was consumed by darkness.

***

When Bekki woke up, the first thing she was aware of was severe pain. She felt as if her entire head was being beaten like a drum from the inside. The more she moved the harder the drumming. Reluctantly, she pushed herself up into a sitting position on the floor. She noticed the notepad was gone. A dazed glance at her watch showed that it was now well after midnight. She had been laying on the floor for hours. Shakily she dialed Nick's phone number. She pressed the phone against her ear and closed her eyes to hold back her tears.

"Please answer," she whispered. As if he had heard her, Nick's voice came on the line.

"Bekki?" he asked sleepily. "Are you okay?"

"Someone attacked me," she murmured breathlessly. Suddenly she was aware that whoever had attacked her was likely Lydia's killer and could easily still be in the house. "Nick please, will you come over?" she asked. "I'm sorry, so sorry, please will you just..."

"I'll be there right over," he assured her. "Are you safe now?"

"I don't know," Bekki admitted fearfully.

"Can you get up?" he asked. She could tell that he was running out of his house. "Can you walk to the door?"

"I think so," Bekki whispered. She carefully got to her feet. She had to hold on to the wall to keep from losing her balance as her head swam with the effects of the blow to it.

"Lock the door," he told her sternly. "Do not answer it for anyone but me."

Bekki turned the lock and leaned her forehead against the front door. Each breath she took was laced with a new throb of her head.

"I'm almost there," he promised her. She could see him crossing the distance between their houses through the small front window. The sight of him running towards her was such a relief that she felt a few tears slip past. She was not normally afraid. She had trained in martial arts when she decided to move to the city, to make sure that she could protect herself. But she had not expected someone to be waiting for her in her home, or to strike her from behind. Nick reached the door and she hurried to unlock it. He pushed the door open and pulled her into his arms for a quick hug. He looked deep into her eyes.

"What happened?"

"I don't know," she shook her head slowly. "I came home and I called you, and then someone hit me from behind, really hard. But that was around seven, I just woke up now," she frowned.

"Stay right here," he told her firmly as he led her to the couch. "I'm sure whoever it was is long gone, but I'm going to check the house."

Bekki nodded and watched as he skillfully drew his gun and stealthily made his way through the rooms of the house. When he was satisfied that there was no one else present, he walked back into the living room, holstering his gun. He pulled out his cell phone and began dialing.

"Who are you calling?" Bekki asked, still feeling groggy.

"I'm calling for a team to come out here and dust for prints, take your statement, and get you to a hospital. Do you know what they took?" he replied putting the phone to his ear and locking eyes with her. There was a deep strain to his expression that Bekki couldn't quite understand.

"No don't do that," she said firmly. "I know who did this. I don't want the police here. They only took one thing."

"Bekki you were attacked, someone broke into your home," Nick pointed out and stepped closer to her. "At the very least you need to be evaluated for a concussion."

"I'm not going to the hospital," Bekki said sternly. "And I'm not giving anyone my statement, other than you, if you're ready to listen this time."

His lips drew into a regretful grimace at her words and she suddenly realized just how guilty he felt.

"I'm sorry," he said swiftly as he crouched down in front of her and laid his hands on her knees. "When you didn't show up for dinner, I was a little upset," he mumbled. "Okay, maybe I was very upset," he corrected when Bekki studied him with disbelief. "So I didn't take your calls right away. When I came home I saw your car in the driveway, so I decided to speak with you face to face. But when I knocked and you didn't answer..." his voice tightened around his words. "I just thought you were upset with me, or sleeping, I never imagined that you were hurt," his eyes misted with tears as they met hers. "I swear Bekki I had no idea."

"I know you didn't," she assured him, touched that it bothered him so deeply. "It's okay."

"No it isn't," he said firmly. "I should have been here to protect you. I should have listened to you about Lydia. Obviously you're on to something."

"I am," she nodded confidently. "But I still don't have any proof. I found the notepad that the suicide note was written on in this woman Julie's motel room."

"What were you doing in her motel room?" Nick questioned, his eyes narrowing.

"Well she came into the salon, and she was missing one of the backs of her earrings, a silver one, like the one I saw at the bakery. Then she told me she was from Chicago, just like Lydia. I just couldn't shake the possibility that she had something to do with Lydia's death."

Nick rocked back on his heels slightly as he nodded. "That was the name you were saying when I came into the salon."

"Yes," Bekki admitted and lowered her eyes slightly. "I knew you wouldn't believe me, so I thought I'd do a little more digging myself. Then I found out that she was a very wealthy woman, married to one of the wealthiest men in Chicago."

"I see," Nick said quietly, offering her no hint of what he thought about her running her own investigation despite him insisting she stay out of it.

"So I decided to just take a little peek in her motel room," Bekki cringed as she spoke the words.

"She invited you in?" Nick asked, meeting her eyes again.

"Not exactly," Bekki replied, not wanting to lie.

"So how did you get in?" he demanded, his tone becoming a little sterner.

"Does that really matter right now?" Bekki shot back. "I found the notepad, and I knew it had to be the same one. I was going to give it to you, but when I closed the salon I noticed that Morris was escorting this woman's husband into the bakery. Morris called him Lydia's son. Then I was certain that Julie had to be involved. I mean, that was the connection between Lydia and Julie."

Nick ran his palms lightly along Bekki's knees as he pondered her words. She could tell that he was not exactly pleased that she had broken into Julie's motel room, but he was piecing the evidence together in his mind.

"So you're saying she was in the bakery, she had the notepad the suicide note came from, and she had a family connection to Lydia," he said calmly.

"Yes, yes, yes!" Bekki said with some excitement, feeling as if Nick was finally catching on.

"Bekki," he sighed as he stared up at her.

"That still doesn't mean Julie killed her."

"What are you talking about?" Bekki demanded. "With all that proof..."

"It's not proof," Nick said firmly. "All you've explained is the reason why Julie was in town was to visit her mother-in-law. She might have let Lydia borrow her notepad or some paper from it, and the back of her earring might have fallen off while she was at the bakery. In fact, Julie's visit might be even more of a reason why Lydia killed herself. Maybe there was some family dispute. Maybe Julie gave her some bad news."

Bekki stared at Nick, her eyes wide, her heart beating so slowly that she was certain she might pass out again. She wanted to argue every point he made, but they actually did make sense.

"But she lied to me, she said she was in town for shopping..." Bekki began to say.

"People lie, Bekki," he said quietly and gave one of her knees a light squeeze. "Just like if I asked you, did you break into Julie's motel room and steal from her, I expect you wouldn't tell me the whole truth."

Bekki froze beneath his scrutiny. The way he described it made her feel as if she was the criminal. Nick held her gaze as he continued, his dark green eyes hardening. "Maybe Julie didn't want to tell you that she had come to town to confront her mother-in-law, or deliver some bad news. So it was easier for her to just say that she was in town for some shopping."

Bekki felt all of her certainty beginning to fade away. Was it possible that she had jumped to several wrong conclusions? Was it possible that Lydia had killed herself after all?

"But then, why would someone attack me?" Bekki pointed out. "Obviously I didn't imagine that," she pointed out sharply.

"Bekki I'm not saying that you imagined it," he insisted, his expression softening. "Listen, the most important thing right now is to make sure that you're okay. If you don't want to make a police report, that's up to you, but I am going to call my friend who is a paramedic and he is going to look you over, understand?" he asked pointedly.

Bekki nodded a little, still reeling with confusion. While Nick placed the call to his friend, Bekki kept hashing over what she had been certain was proof. She was beginning to realize that Nick's job was a lot harder than it looked. Within a few minutes his friend arrived.

"This is Paul," Nick introduced him casually. "Paul this is..." Nick hesitated for a second as if he wasn't sure how to introduce Bekki.

"I'm Bekki," she interjected and offered him a tight smile. "And I'm fine."

"Let's see that bump, hmm?" Paul asked. He looked as if he was in his forties and had a gentle demeanor about him. She leaned forward slightly and swept her dark hair aside so that he could see the back of her neck. Paul offered a low whistle.

"That's some bump," he said quietly and glanced at Nick. "How did this happen?"

"She was hit from behind," Nick explained.

"Must have been with something pretty heavy," Paul clucked his tongue. "Luckily it doesn't look like it did any internal damage. But she should have an MRI to rule it out," he shone a small penlight in Bekki's eyes and watched their reaction. "Honestly, she should get checked out at the hospital to be certain, but it looks like she handled the blow well. Alternating heat and ice over the next few hours should bring the bump down," he frowned as he turned back to Bekki. "I'm sorry this happened to you."

"Me too," Bekki winced as she rubbed at the back of her neck.

"Thanks Paul," Nick said as his friend packed up his medical kit. "I'll get her to the hospital right away."

"You'll do no such thing," Bekki insisted as she shifted her head from side to side. "I'm fine Nick. I'll just ice it."

Nick pursed his lips and looked back at Paul. "You have anything in that kit for stubbornness?"

Paul laughed and shook his head. "I wouldn't recommend her being alone tonight, just in case the pain gets worse or she experiences dizziness or weakness."

'Oh don't worry, she won't be alone," Nick assured him as he walked Paul to the door. Once his friend was gone Nick walked back into the living room. He stared hard at Bekki who was hunched over on the couch.

"What am I going to do with you?" he asked with a half smile.

"Nurse me back to health I hope," she smiled sweetly in return.

"Gladly," he replied. "Just rest a moment, I'll get some ice from the kitchen."

Bekki nodded and listened as he rummaged through the freezer. He returned with a carefully wrapped ice pack. When he sat down on the couch beside her, she scooted closer to him. She rested her head lightly on his shoulder. When his lips grazed her forehead in a subtle kiss she felt her body begin to relax. His presence was such a comfort to her, even if he didn't agree with her theories. He leaned back against the couch, and laid a pillow in his lap.

"Just rest," he encouraged her and guided her head down to the pillow. He grabbed the ice pack from the table beside the couch and rested it gingerly against the area above her neck where she had been struck.

"Are you upset with me still?" she asked in a whisper as she peeked up at him.

"About what?" he asked with a furrowed brow.

"Me standing you up for dinner," she replied.

"No," he shook his head and drew a heavy breath. "I was just disappointed. I was looking forward to having some time to talk with you."

As his fingers trailed down through her hair she was amazed by how comfortable she was snuggled up to him. It seemed as if it didn't matter if they agreed with one another, or even if they got along. All that mattered was that they were close to one another.

"I'm here now," she said quietly.

"Now's not the time," he said sternly and frowned as he studied her eyes intently.

"So it wasn't going to be a good talk?" she asked curiously, her heart sinking.

Nick sighed and smiled faintly as he watched her expression shift. "Sometimes I think you missed your calling, you're a great interrogator."

"Thanks," Bekki said with a smile.

"I just think there's some things, we should discuss," he explained cryptically.

"Like what?" she wondered, her breath caught in her chest.

"Like, the past, and maybe the future," he said carefully.

"You mean when we were kids?" Bekki laughed dismissively.

He curved a hand lightly along her cheek, and stroked his thumb across her cheekbone.

"Was that really all it was to you?" he asked in a whisper. "Just kid stuff?"

Bekki's heart began thumping loudly. She knew she should be thinking about Lydia, figuring out the truth. But with the questions Nick was asking she couldn't focus on anything but the desire she felt within her.

"Isn't that what it was?" she asked hesitantly. "I mean," she paused a moment, swallowed thickly, and then boldly met his gaze. "You didn't even say goodbye, Nick."

His eyes widened at her words and his face grew slightly pale. "Is that what you thought all this time?"

"It's what happened," Bekki pointed out as she

narrowed her eyes. "One minute we were, together..."

"In love," he corrected, his eyes heavy on hers.

"The next minute you were gone," she said with determination, not letting his claim of love distract her. It was just a high school romance, she tried to scream at herself within her mind.

"I was gone because my Grandfather died," Nick explained. "It happened so suddenly that my parents just took off, hoping to get to the hospital before he passed. They stayed long enough for the funeral, and then I stayed behind with my uncle and some of my cousins to help my grandmother straighten out and fix up the house."

"You could have called," she pointed out with a frown.

"I did call," he said quickly. "I called a dozen times, but you never answered."

Bekki cringed as she remembered dropping her phone in a friend's pool and having to get a new number. Nick didn't have his own phone, and she had no way of contacting him, or even knowing where he was. "I thought you were angry with me," he explained. "I thought you wanted nothing to do with me. So I wrote you a letter. I told you how I felt, how much I cared about you, and that if I did something to upset you I was sorry. I asked if you felt the same way, and that if you didn't it was okay, I wouldn't bring it up again. But you never wrote me back," he studied her, a shadow of hurt darkening his eyes.

"That's because I never got the letter," Bekki groaned and turned her face into the firmness of his chest. She couldn't believe that a heartbreak that had been following her for nearly her entire life had been a complete mistake.

"When I got back, and you didn't want anything to do with me..."

"Because I thought you left without saying goodbye," Bekki reminded him.

"I just thought I had to move on," he admitted with a slight nod. "I thought that was what you wanted."

"It was never what I wanted," she pursed her lips slightly and peeked up at him. "That summer was the best time in my life."

"Mine too," he replied quietly. "So maybe we can start over?" he suggested hopefully.

"I don't know," Bekki said as she slowly sat up. He placed the ice pack back on the table beside the couch and looked over at her.

"Why? Isn't it worth seeing if we still feel the same way?" he asked, his eyes not leaving hers.

Bekki felt her chest tighten. She already knew she felt the same way. If she was honest with herself she had never stopped feeling the same way.

"We're not kids anymore Nick," she reminded him. "We've both lived our lives, and grown up, and changed."

"All the more reason to get to know each other again," he said as he curled his arm around her waist and pulled her back closer to him as gently as he could. "Don't tell me you don't feel it too Bekki, because that night in the truck…"

"I know," Bekki breathed. "It's not that I don't want to Nick. I just don't want to give you the wrong idea."

"What idea is that?" he inquired his

questioning persistent.

"That I'm ready for anything serious," she explained hesitantly.

"This is about Trevor, isn't it?" he asked with a sigh.

"That has something to do with it," she admitted. "Like you told me about Lydia, you think you know someone..."

"But that's the point Bekki," he grasped one of her hands gently in his own. "All I'm asking for is the chance to get to know you again. I don't need you to protect me, I'm a big boy, and I know the risk. I just want the opportunity to see where this could go."

Bekki smiled a little at his words. She had been hoping he wanted just that, but it was still hard for her to think of getting back into a relationship after the betrayal she had felt when Trevor cheated on her.

"Well, in that case Detective," Bekki offered a subtle smile. "I did break into Julie's room. And I still think Lydia didn't kill herself. And I'm not going to stop until I find out who did it," she said sternly. "That's who I am. Are you sure that's who you want to get to know?"

'Positive," he replied and leaned in for a sensual kiss. When he pulled away, he tugged her back down into his lap. "After you get a little rest."

Bekki yawned as the late hour insisted she sleep at least a little. She settled back against him and smiled as she felt Nick's arms wrap around her. In his grasp she felt safe. She drifted right off to sleep.

***

It seemed as if only minutes had passed, but in truth Bekki had been sleeping for hours. She woke to the smell of coffee, and a piercing headache. She groaned as she slowly sat up. As soon as she saw that she was laying in her bed, her heart skipped a beat. Nick must have carried her into the room while she was sleeping. It made her feel a million different ways at once to think that she had slept so deeply that she didn't even notice. Had he slept beside her? She couldn't tell from the ruffled blankets.

"Coffee?" Nick asked as he leaned against the doorway of the bedroom. Bekki shifted uncomfortably in the bed.

"No thanks, I think I just need some Aspirin," she winced as she reached around to touch the back of her neck.

"Here let me take a look," he said as he sat down on the bed beside her. She held her breath as his fingertips coasted along the slope of her neck and his body leaned closer to hers. He began to rub softly beneath the small knot that was still on her neck. His soothing touch eased some of the shooting pain she was feeling.

"That's nice," she sighed and leaned back into his caresses. "So are we going to arrest her today?"

"We are not arresting anyone," he reminded her. "I'm the one with the handcuffs. And no, we don't have enough evidence to do that. Since you wouldn't let me call in the team to process the scene, we have nothing to arrest her for."

"Seriously?" Bekki sighed with frustration.

"Hey, don't ruin all my hard work here," he said sharply and moved his hands over her shoulders to massage them.

"Well, I guess I'll just go into the salon then," Bekki sighed.

"No you won't," he corrected her. "Sammy is running the salon. You're staying home, and resting, and staying out of trouble."

"Do you really think that's possible?" she asked with a wry smile.

"No, but I'm still going to tell you that's what you should be doing," he answered, hiding a smile which quickly faded. "I mean it Bekki. Somebody attacked you last night. If it were up to me I'd put a car on you, but I know you wouldn't like that."

"You're right about that," Bekki frowned.

"So please just let me do my job and stay in bed?" he suggested.

"Well, if you promise to give me another massage later, maybe," Bekki nodded a little. She felt as if she could sleep for hours.

"Good," he kissed the top of her head gently. "I'll call you with an update, okay?"

She nodded and smiled as he left the room.

"Thanks Nick!" she called after him.

She lay back in the bed and as soon as she did she was reminded of her need for Aspirin. Nick had already left, so she went to the bathroom to search for a bottle. Nothing there. Nothing in the kitchen.

"Ugh," Bekki winced as her head pounded. She was just going to have to go to the store and get some. After she dressed she decided it would be best to walk into town. She didn't trust herself to drive after a blow to the head. When she reached the store she bought the biggest bottle of Aspirin she could find and a bottle of water to go with it. After taking two and washing them down with a gulp of water she walked back out of the store and into the town square. That was when she spotted Julie. She had just left the local diner and was staring hard at her phone. Bekki knew she should just head straight back home, but she couldn't. She wanted to know exactly what Julie was up to. As she trailed after her, the woman continued to stare hard at her phone. She wasn't texting, or playing a game, it was almost as if she was looking at a map.

Bekki crept close enough to her to catch a

glimpse of the app she was looking at. It was a map, with a blinking red icon. It looked like a GPS. Bekki hung back, not wanting Julie to realize she was there. She followed Julie all the way to the edge of the lake. When the woman paused, Bekki did too, a few feet away. She ducked behind a bush, and looked past Julie at the water.

A very tall and handsome man stood at the edge of the water with his hands shoved deep into his pockets. He was dwarfed by the lake spreading out before him, making him appear quite young and vulnerable. No one stood with him, and he didn't seem to be in any hurry to turn away from the natural beauty. His shoulders were slumped. Bekki was a little too far away to be sure, but she thought they were trembling. Bekki realized that Julie must have been using a tracking app. It was probably linked to Dan's phone.

"Daniel," Julie said as she stepped up behind him. Bekki's nostrils flared with anger as she realized that the woman who she suspected had killed Daniel's mother was about to embrace him.

"Julie," he said with surprise as he spun around to face her. "What are you doing here?" he frowned, his eyes narrowed. He did not seem terribly happy to see her.

"I heard about your mother," she said quietly and stepped a little closer to him. "I'm so sorry, Daniel, I know how deeply you loved her. I just didn't want you to be alone at a time like this," she reached out and gently grasped his forearm.

Dan's expression hardened as he studied her. It was clear that whatever problems had arose in their marriage were not ones he was willing to forgive. However, in the next moment Julie slid her arms around his waist and hugged him, pressing her body close.

"Please Daniel, I know this past year has been difficult, I know that you hate me, but don't shut me out now. I know you need someone," she purred her words and looked up at him pleadingly.

Bekki shuddered with disgust as she thought about what she believed this woman had done to Lydia, and now she was heartless enough to try to offer comfort to her son? Dan didn't have any idea that his mother's death had been anything other than suicide, however, and certainly no notion that his soon to be ex-wife could have somehow been involved. So he hugged her in return, and rested his chin against the top of her perfectly coiffed head.

"Julie, I just don't understand it. If she was upset about something, why didn't she just come to me? Why didn't she just ask for help?"

Julie sighed and closed her eyes as she hugged him tighter. "That's something we may never know Dan. She was a good woman, but she held a lot of things inside. Maybe she had her own secrets."

"Maybe," Dan nodded a little. "But it still seems so impossible."

Bekki leaned her head back against the side of a canoe shelter as she listened to their conversation. She wanted to jump out and accuse Julie right then, but she remembered what Nick said. There was still a possibility that Julie had nothing to do with Lydia's death at all. But why was she in town, before Dan arrived? Was it still possible that something she had said during a visit with Lydia had upset her to such a degree that Lydia had decided to kill herself? As she watched Dan's large frame envelop the rather petite Julie, another damning thought occurred to Bekki. If Julie did kill Lydia, how did she get her body up and into the noose? She didn't look strong enough to pull off something like that. Bekki decided it was time to return to the scene of the crime, and start from the beginning again. But she needed to make sure she did so on her own.

As she was walking back towards the bakery she stopped short. Nick's car was parked in front of it. Bekki ducked behind a building, hoping that he hadn't seen her, doing exactly what he had asked her not to do. She nearly jumped out of her skin when her phone rang. Had he seen her? She peeked at the phone and saw that it was indeed Nick calling. She reluctantly answered.

"Hi," she said quietly.

"Hey, did I wake you?" he asked, sounding as if he was very concerned.

"No," Bekki replied, her eyes widening with relief as she realized that he hadn't actually seen her. He was just calling to check in. "I was just resting," she bit the end of her tongue lightly and hoped he wouldn't be able to tell that she was lying.

"Good, make sure you keep doing that, okay?" he asked.

"Of course," Bekki cringed.

"Listen, I have some more information on Daniel Brentwood and Julie," he said quickly.

Bekki peeked around the corner of the building and saw Nick pacing back and forth in front of his car. She ducked back behind the building.

"Oh what is it?" she asked and started walking in the other direction.

"It seems they're in the middle of a very messy divorce. They both have high paid lawyers, and let's just say it's not exactly amicable."

"Well, that might be why she attacked Lydia," Bekki said carefully, trying to disguise the fact that she was walking.

"If she did," Nick reminded her. "But you're right. There's some bad blood there. Apparently Lydia and Julie even had a very public argument over Dan at a restaurant. Lydia accused Julie of being after her son's money, and it turned into a big media frenzy."

"I bet," Bekki shook her head. She could easily imagine Lydia calling Julie out in front of a crowd of people. "No wonder she was holed up here."

"Exactly," Nick said. "I'll let you know if I find out anything new, all right?"

"Thanks Nick," she smiled into the phone.

"Bekki, make sure you're resting. Don't answer the door for anyone, got me?" he said sternly.

"I know, I know," Bekki insisted and ducked down one of the side streets that would lead back to Rose Hill Drive.

"Call me if you need anything," he insisted.

"I will Nick, thanks again," Bekki hung up the phone swiftly. By the time she reached her house she was tired. Since Nick was at the bakery she'd have to wait until later to look it over again. She decided to lay down and rest for a little while. However, as she closed her eyes all she could see was Julie wrapping her arms around Dan. The poor guy had no idea what kind of woman he was married to. The very idea of Julie getting away with the horrible crime haunted her so deeply that she could not sleep. Within an hour she was awake again and ready to do some real investigation work. She called Nick's cell to get an idea of where he was.

"What are you up to?" she asked when he answered.

"I'm on my way to you, with the dinner you missed," he replied with a gleeful tone. Bekki bit her lip to keep from groaning. She was going to be stuck sharing dinner with Nick. "Bekki, are you all right?" he asked when she was quiet for so long.

"Sure, I'm just a little tired," Bekki explained. "I was going to sleep for a while."

"Well you have to eat too," he said firmly. "I'll be there in a few minutes. As long as you take a few bites, I'll leave you alone."

"All right," Bekki smiled a little at how sweet he was being. It was nice of him to look out for her with such dedication.

When Nick arrived he spread their feast out on the dining room table. It was an Italian dinner of ravioli from the local restaurant, one of Bekki's favorites.

"Mmm, that smells great," she grinned as she picked up a fork.

"So did you actually get any rest today?" Nick asked as she began devouring her portion of ravioli.

"Some," Bekki nodded. "It's hard for me to sleep, knowing what happened to Lydia."

"Just remember Bekki, Julie is innocent until proven guilty. Sometimes things look very different to what they actually are."

"Maybe," Bekki shrugged slightly. She didn't want to argue with him. He didn't have to be certain, but she was. As they finished their meal Nick started clearing away the take out containers.

"Are you sure you don't want me to stay with you?" he asked a little nervously as he tossed the boxes and plates in the trash.

"No, I don't know if I could sleep with you next to me," she said slyly as he sat back in his chair.

"I slept on the couch," he said quickly, blushing a little.

"Oh," Bekki felt a little disappointed. She had enjoyed imagining him laying beside her. "Well, maybe when I'm feeling better we can make this a real dinner out, hmm?"

"I'd love that," he agreed and then paused beside her. "If anything happens tonight, just give me a call. I'll be at home only a few minutes away," he reminded her.

"Thanks Nick, for everything," she smiled. When they kissed she felt a ripple of desire that almost convinced her to forget about searching the bakery. But she couldn't. She pulled away from him and yawned, as if she was exhausted.

"All right, you head to bed," he murmured reluctantly. Apparently he had felt the same pull.

"I'm going," Bekki assured him. She walked into the bedroom and lay down. Then she listened for the door to close behind him. She waited until the sun had fully set and then climbed right back out of bed. She peered through the front window but she couldn't see him. She knew she had to be careful not to be spotted. She slipped out through the back door, and headed straight for the bakery.

Chapter Four

The bakery was dark except for the natural light of the moon filtering through the front window which illuminated enough of the front of the store for Bekki to look around. She knew that the moment Nick found out she had snuck into the bakery, he would be livid, but as she had told him, this was who she was. She was not going to let a silly thing like trespassing stop her from discovering the truth. A hair pin had made the lock very easy to open. As she studied the room around her she began to imagine what Lydia's last moments might have been like. Maybe she and Julie were arguing. Maybe Julie had drugged her so that she would be easier to kill. But Nick had claimed that the toxins screen they ran on her, to rule out any influence of drugs or alcohol, was clear. So Lydia, a relatively strong woman, and Julie, a thin but powerful woman, were arguing in the front of the bakery. How did that argument transform into a murder that looked like a suicide? It just didn't make sense. She could not figure out how Lydia ended up hanged in her own bakery.

Of course the noose had been cut down from the rafter. But Bekki wanted to recreate the crime scene as much as possible. It had been burned into her mind, but still, she might have overlooked something. Bekki pulled a chair back under the spot where Lydia had been found. She tested its sturdiness. Then she climbed on top of it. From her perspective she could see the entire front of the bakery. She was slightly shorter than Lydia had been, but not enough to make a big difference. She stood on her toes, imagining the noose around her neck. It was an eerie thing to think of, even if she knew it wasn't going to happen to her. She couldn't imagine how it must have felt for Lydia.

"Then she kicked it out from under her," Bekki said under her breath as she tried to figure out the sequence of events. "That's what she would have had to do if she killed herself."

Bekki's eyes glanced down in the direction of the floor. She remembered where the suicide note had been. She could tell that Lydia would have been able to look right at it. In fact, the words were positioned facing her, so that she could have read it.

"Lydia, why would you want to look at the note?" she asked out loud, her voice filling the empty bakery.

Bekki frowned and then stepped down from the chair. This time instead of imagining the suicide, she envisioned the murder.

"Julie, what are you doing here?" she asked, as if the woman had walked up behind her.

Perhaps Julie had threatened her. Perhaps she had simply attacked her. She was certain there would have been a lot of anger.

"No, that isn't right," she frowned. "Lydia had no bruises or scratches on her. But if she wasn't drugged, if she wasn't beaten, then how did Julie get her into the noose?"

"Excuse me?" a voice said sharply from behind the counter of the bakery. "Just who are you, and what are you doing in my mother's bakery?" Dan demanded as he walked swiftly around the counter towards Bekki. Bekki's eyes widened as she recognized him. Her heart pounded. Dan had seemed so upset, but there was still a chance that he had something to do with his mother's death as well. He would certainly have been strong enough to help his wife.

"I'm Bekki," she said quickly and stepped back away from him. Dan's eyes flashed with annoyance.

"What are you doing in here? Why were you saying those things about my mother and my wife?" he looked quite menacing as he drew closer to her.

"I'm so sorry," Bekki said quickly. "I knew your mother, and I just, I just couldn't picture her taking her own life."

He paused a moment as if her words had struck a chord with him, but then his anger swiftly returned.

"And that gives you the right to break in here and imagine such horrible things about my wife?" he asked. "What did you mean by, how did Julie get her into the noose?"

Bekki shivered as she realized how much trouble she had gotten herself into. Not only had she been caught trespassing, and truly breaking and entering, but she had also openly accused Dan's wife of murder with no proof whatsoever.

"I didn't mean anything," she insisted, her panic growing. "I'll leave right now. I'm sorry to disturb you," she started to move towards the door but the moment she did, Dan stepped in front of her and pulled out his cell phone.

"Oh no, you won't. You're not going anywhere. You broke in here, and you're accusing my wife of horrible things. We'll let the police deal with this," as he dialed, Bekki felt her heart sink. Her attempt at being clandestine had certainly not worked out very well. Nick was not going to be pleased that she had lied, yet again, about what she was up to. Worse than that, it might not be Nick at all who came to the scene. To any other police officer this would look like a simple case of breaking and entering, and she would have no chance of defending herself. But maybe that would be better than Nick being the one to walk through the door. She closed her eyes and imagined the exact look that would be on Nick's face. He wouldn't be able to sweep this under the rug.

***

The police station was relatively calm. It was Nick's night to catch up on some paperwork, but his mind kept wandering back to the case. He had sent the suicide note for handwriting analysis, despite the trouble he could get into for investigating a closed case. He just could not shake Bekki's insistence that something was not right about the case. He also wanted to figure out who might have attacked her in order to get the notepad back. The last thing he wanted was for her to be in danger. A part of him hoped it wasn't true. That the case was as simple as it seemed. But he had begun to trust Bekki's instincts.

Nick's partner, Detective Williams, paused beside his desk and knocked lightly on it.

"Just thought I'd give you a heads up," she frowned. "Your little amateur detective got herself into some serious trouble again," she sighed and rolled her eyes. "I intercepted the call, and told the uniforms that you would take care of it. But you better get out there fast. Sounds like she broke into the bakery, and Lydia's son caught her."

"You can't be serious?" Nick sighed as he wiped a hand across his face. "I can't believe she did it again."

"I am serious," she replied and leaned a little

closer to Nick. "Look, she may seem pretty sharp but you've got a good reputation right now Nick. If you keep covering for her, you could lose it, and even your job," her tone was full of warning as she added. "I won't get involved again."

Nick nodded and drew his fingertips along his temples. He knew that she was putting her own job at risk by interfering.

"I know, thanks," he frowned and stood up from his desk.

"I mean it Nick, you need to get a handle on this situation," she insisted.

"I know, I know," he repeated, his heart pounding harder with each word he spoke. As he grabbed his jacket and headed for the door anyone watching would have been certain that he was a man on a mission.

***

Waiting in the bakery for the police to arrive was tedious for Bekki. She knew that she would have no good explanation to offer. She had to come up with some reason why she was there. If she didn't she might find herself spending the night in jail. Dan was standing sullenly beside the counter, doing his best to ignore her. Bekki decided to try to reason with him. Maybe he would let her leave before the police arrived.

"Listen, I didn't mean to upset you," Bekki assured Dan. "I didn't think anyone would be here. I just wanted to help."

"Well, you didn't," he shot back with a stormy expression. He had begun pacing back and forth as he waited for the police to arrive. His eyes kept traveling back to the chair that Bekki had placed back in the center of the room. "You think it helps to see that?" he gasped out and shook his head. As his shoulders began to shake Bekki realized that he was not as angry as he was sorrowful.

"I'm sorry," she said again and took a step towards him. She truly did regret causing all of his pain to be stirred up by the way she had set up the scene. For just an instant she wondered what might happen if she turned out to be wrong.

"Don't," he warned her. "Please. I just need all of this to be over with. The media is going to have a field day with it. I have her funeral to plan. I just can't take anything else," he said with frustration. "I just want to get my wife and myself out of this little town," he shot a disgusted glare through the front window of the bakery.

Bekki stared hard at the floor as she realized she had caused him more pain than he was already in. Even if she did find out the truth, it would not necessarily make things better for him. Could he survive knowing that his wife had killed his own mother? What if she didn't find the proof she needed? Could she just let Dan walk away, knowing that he was married to a murderer? Bekki fell silent as she resigned herself to waiting for the police to arrive. She could only hope that she would not end up in handcuffs.

***

When Nick stepped into the bakery Bekki sighed with relief. But when he turned his professional glare on to her, she cringed and realized he might not be able to protect her this time.

"What seems to be the problem?" he asked Dan, his words careful.

"This woman broke in here," Dan said sternly

and pointed an accusing finger at Bekki.

"Nick I..." Bekki started to speak.

Nick snapped his gaze towards her before she could continue. "Not a word," he warned and then pointed at the wall. "You, against the wall."

Bekki's lips parted to protest but Nick's intense gaze made it clear that she needed to do as he instructed.

"What's going on here?" Dan demanded as he looked between the two. "Do you know her?"

Bekki bit into her bottom lip to keep from offering yet another explanation, or more likely another lie. She reluctantly rested her shoulders against the wall, and watched as Nick turned back to Dan.

"I'm sorry if there's been some confusion here tonight," he began carefully. "Bekki, as you may be aware runs the local salon."

"And?" Dan asked with annoyance. "What does that have to do with her breaking in here?"

"She knew your mother quite well," Nick explained patiently, as if he was trying to reason with the man, "and had asked her to bake a special cake for her friend's birthday. I'm sure she was just here, hoping to get the cake. Weren't you Bekki?" he asked without turning to look at her.

"Yes, of course," Bekki gasped out. She was very impressed with Nick's quick thinking, but she also knew it had to be going against his moral compass to be fabricating a story to cover for her illegal actions. "I just didn't want to sound crass by asking you for it, I'm sorry. I know I shouldn't have come, but it's for a very good friend of mine, and I didn't want to see it go to waste."

'A cake?" Dan said skeptically. "Then why were you accusing my wife of horrible things? Why did you put this chair here?" he demanded, his rage resurfacing swiftly.

"I'm not sure what you mean," Bekki said quietly. "There are some rumors going around town. Working where I do, I hear them all. I was just saying them out loud. I guess, I just didn't believe that what happened could be true."

"Well, this isn't some piece of gossip to feast on," Dan hissed. "My mother is dead, she's gone, and you and this entire tiny town seem to think it's just something to talk about."

"It's not that at all," Bekki insisted, her voice softening. "It's just that everyone who knew your mother cared about her."

Dan still did not look pleased but Nick planted himself firmly between Dan and Bekki.

"I'll tell you what Dan, I'll take her over to the station, question her a little further, and you can decide if you want to press charges," he said with a mild shrug.

Bekki held her breath, wondering if Nick really would arrest her. He was pulling handcuffs off of his belt, and she knew they were meant for her.

Dan sighed and reluctantly shook his head. "Look, I've been a bit overwhelmed by all of this. She didn't steal anything, and she didn't break anything. Maybe we can let it go."

"Are you sure?" Nick asked with concern. "I want you to know that our entire community is here to help you with whatever you need."

"I appreciate that," Dan said quietly. Then he looked past Nick to where Bekki was still standing against the wall. "Just keep her away from me, and my wife, and everything should be fine."

"No problem," Nick assured him with a polite smile. "Rebekah?" he summoned her and she winced at the use of her full name. Bekki walked towards him slowly, each step feeling as if she was delivering herself to her judge and jury.

"I'm sorry again Dan," she said with genuine remorse. The last thing she wanted to do was cause him more pain. Nick was obviously tense as she stood beside him. She could tell his patience was running thin.

"Just, do me a favor, and stay out of my business," Dan said, his tone short. "I don't need a media frenzy right now. I just need some time to say goodbye."

Bekki nodded, but she knew that she couldn't promise him. She knew that with everything she had discovered she could not simply let this go.

When she felt Nick's hand curl around her elbow she could tell from the tension of his grasp that he had quite a bit to say to her about the incident. He steered her out of the bakery and around to the parking lot behind it where his car was parked. He was silent as he opened the passenger side door to his car.

"Oh it's a nice night, I could walk," Bekki said lightly and started to pull away from him. He settled his gaze on her with absolutely no compassion, and she felt her next words stick in her throat. She recalled his extreme sense of justice, and his belief that breaking the law was never justified. Maybe he was still going to take her to the station, just to make a point. He continued to hold the door open for her. Feeling a sense of dread rise within her, Bekki slumped into the seat. He closed the door sharply behind her and walked around to the front of the car. As he was opening the door, his cell phone began to ring. He shot her a look of warning, and then answered the phone.

"Malonie," he said with more animosity than was meant for the caller. "Are you certain?" he asked with a slightly milder tone. "Make sure you have that information on my desk by the morning. Right, yes, we'll need to change the status of the case. Thank you."

He hung up the phone and slid into the

driver's seat of the car. He tossed his phone into the console between the seats and grasped the steering wheel so tightly that his knuckles turned white as the skin pulled taut.

"Can you please tell me one thing Bekki?" he asked through gritted teeth. Bekki braced herself, prepared for a lecture, or worse, for Nick to make it clear that he wanted nothing to do with her.

"Anything," she agreed nervously.

"How is it that you are always right?" he demanded and shot a glare in her direction.

"Nick it's not what you think..." she started to defend herself, and then blinked slowly. "Wait, what did you say?"

"You heard me," Nick said smacking the heel of his palm against the steering wheel. "How am I supposed to get it through your head that what you're doing is wrong, if it always turns out to be right?"

Bekki fell silent as she wondered just what kind of game he was playing. Was he trying to get her to confess something? Was it some kind of trick?

"Well?" Nick asked again. "Any explanation?" he narrowed his eyes.

"I just like to get to the truth," Bekki said quietly.

"I see that," Nick nodded and wiped his hand across his face, rubbing lightly at his eyes as he did. "I sent in the note for handwriting analysis. I just got the results."

"Oh?" Bekki asked.

"The note was forged Bekki, it wasn't written by Lydia," he shook his head in disbelief. "You were so sure this whole time."

Bekki was silent as her heart thumped against her chest. "Can they tell who wrote it?"

"Not without a sample to compare it to," Nick explained. "But it certainly means that the case will be looked at more closely now. Thanks to you we already have a suspect."

"Why does it seem like that doesn't make you happy?" Bekki asked hesitantly.

He sighed and stared through the windshield. "Bekki I just don't want you to put yourself in these dangerous situations. What if it hadn't been Dan that walked in? What if it had been Julie? Do you think you're immune to danger?"

Bekki shook her head. "Of course not. But I can take care of myself, Nick," she said firmly.

"Until you can't," he said sharply. "Then what? I'll be showing up to investigate?"

"Nick, I was never in any danger," Bekki said, her eyes narrowed with determination. "Lydia was the one who was in danger, and no one was there to help her. No one was there to stop it from happening."

"What makes you so different from Lydia, Bekki?" his voice raised some as he struck the steering wheel hard with his palm again. "That's my point. What makes you different from her?"

Bekki sat back in her seat, a little startled by his anger. She lifted her eyes to his and spoke with pure confidence.

"I have you."

Nick grumbled and tightened his lips into an even line, but she could see the warmth rising in his eyes. "Well, I guess we should get back in there and start an investigation," he sighed.

"We?" Bekki asked hopefully.

"Yes we," he reached over and gave her hand a gentle squeeze.

***

Nick knocked on the front door of the bakery, but no one answered. The door was locked.

"Dan must have left," he frowned. "I'll have to get someone over here to open the door," he pulled out his cell phone.

"Or..." Bekki drew out her word with a subtle smile.

"Or," he frowned and then rolled her eyes. "All right fine, but just this once." Bekki smiled and deftly withdrew the hair pin she had recently discovered doubled very well as a lock pick. She fiddled with the knob until the lock gave way.

"You really are good at that," Nick said begrudgingly.

"One of my many talents," Bekki quipped and swung the door open. As they stepped inside Nick flipped the light switch on. He shoved his hands deep into his pockets as he studied what was left of the scene.

"Lydia really was murdered," he said solemnly. "You were right all along, I really thought it was a suicide."

Bekki was silent as she stared into space. She still could not comprehend how Lydia had ended up in the noose. How could a person be murdered and have only what appeared to be self-inflicted wounds?

As if taking the thoughts right out of her mind Nick shook his head. "Someone had to be really sick to do this Bekki," he turned to look her straight in the eye. "This is why I ask you to stay out of things like this. If it really was Julie that did this, who knows what else she might be capable of," as his lecture continued Bekki could barely hear him. Her eyes were slowly widening as a horrible thought formed.

"You're right," she whispered again, tears beginning to fill her eyes as she stared at the empty chair in front of her still positioned right beneath the area where the noose had hung.

"Bekki," he reached out to grasp her shoulder gently when he saw the tears. "Don't cry, please, I don't mean to frighten you."

"No, it's not that," Bekki shook her head slightly. "I mean you're right, Lydia did kill herself."

"No," he shook his head. "Didn't you hear me Bekki? The handwriting analysis came back, it doesn't match Lydia's. Someone forged the suicide note."

"Oh yes they did," Bekki nodded as she reached up to wipe at her eyes. "But Lydia still killed herself."

"I don't understand," Nick frowned. "Did you figure something out?"

"There was one piece I couldn't understand," she explained. "How did Julie get Lydia into the noose. She couldn't lift her, she didn't drug her, so how did she do it?"

"I don't know," Nick shook his head. "Forensics is going to have a hard time figuring it out, since the crime scene has already been compromised."

"She made her," Bekki uttered, absolutely horrified by the idea. "She made her do it herself."

"How? How could someone force someone to do something like that?" he asked, scratching at his light brown hair.

"There's only one way, and there's no way to prove it," Bekki felt her horror transform into hopelessness as she murmured her next words. "She's going to get away with it, isn't she Nick?"

Nick slid his arm around her shoulders and studied her intently. "Not with you on the case Bekki," he said firmly. She took a deep breath and felt her resolve to capture Lydia's murderer return. Maybe there would be no evidence to prove her claim. But evidence wasn't the only way to get a conviction. A confession could be just as damning.

"I'm going to go," Bekki said suddenly as she walked towards the door.

"Bekki wait," Nick followed after her. "I don't want you to be alone. If this woman already knows that you're on to her and finds out that we suspect her, she may come after you again."

"I can take care of myself Nick," Bekki said sternly. "I'll be careful."

"She's going to try to confront you," Nick

frowned. "She'll wait until you're alone."

"That's what I'm counting on," Bekki said under her breath.

"What was that?" Nick asked, as he did not hear her clearly.

"Nothing, I just said I would be very careful. I have my phone. I'll call you the minute I sense any danger, okay?" she smiled a little at him. "Remember, I'm always right."

"Until you're wrong," he warned her with one furrowed brow.

"I'll be careful," she assured him a final time. "You see what you can figure out here, I have an idea I need to follow up on."

"Call me," he reminded her as she stepped out of the bakery. As the door fell shut behind her she caught a glimpse of him through the window. She could tell from his expression that he was not at all convinced she would be safe. She was surprised that he let her leave.

Chapter Five

Bekki hurried across the street to the salon. She ducked inside and kept the lights out so that no one would notice she was there. She began digging through the drawers in the reception desk. She knew exactly what she was looking for. Bekki had found that having a voice recorder around when you needed it could be very helpful. The only problem was, she was having a hard time finding it.

"Aha!" she smiled as she closed her hand around the device in the bottom of the lowest drawer. She pulled it out and flipped it over to put in fresh batteries. Once she had it stowed safely in her pocket she sat down at the desk to consider her options. She knew with Dan being suspicious of her, and Julie likely knowing that Bekki was aware of what she had done, the entire situation was going to be quite complicated. Bekki needed to find a way to contact Julie without alerting Dan. She recalled the app that Julie had been using to track Dan, and an idea formed in her mind. She knew that Dan was now staying with Julie at the Harroway Harbor motel.

As she sneaked out the back of the salon she knew that Nick would not approve of what she was about to do, but as long as it worked out the way she hoped, it would be worth the risk in the end. When she arrived at the motel most of the staff were gone for the day. The front desk was empty. Using her cell phone she called the number of the hotel and selected room nine. She waited a few moments, but no one answered. She crept closer to the room and called again. This time she could hear the phone ringing inside the room. She also heard a frustrated huff.

"Answer it, just see who it is," Dan's voice demanded.

"Who would be calling us here?" Julie protested. "It's probably a wrong number."

"It could be the police," Dan pointed out.

"They have your cell phone number," Julie reminded him. Bekki hung up, and then blocked her phone number before calling Dan's cell phone.

"See it is them," Dan said. "Hello?"

Bekki hung up the phone. Then she called back immediately.

"Hello?" Dan said with more frustration.

Bekki hung up right away. Then she called once more. When she did, she heard the frustration in Dan's voice.

"This place must have terrible reception," he said as his phone began ringing again. "Obviously it's important. I'm going to take it outside."

"Don't be long," Julie called after him.

Bekki hurried back out of the motel before Dan could spot her in the hallway. She waited out of sight at the corner of the motel as Dan walked back out. This time when she called his cell phone, she didn't hang up. Instead she disguised her voice.

"Is this Daniel Brentwood?" she asked in a more nasally tone.

"Yes it is," he replied.

"This is Harroway PD, we need you to answer a few questions for us," she made her voice fade in and out as if the connection was bad.

"I'm sorry I can barely hear you. My phone isn't working well. I'll just meet you at the station," he growled with annoyance at his phone as he hung up. Bekki watched as he shoved it into his jacket pocket. Then he headed straight for his car. She waited until he had the door open before jogging out to meet him.

"Hi Dan, remember me?" she said with a cheerful disposition.

"Of course I remember you," he glared at Bekki. "Aren't you supposed to be staying away from me?"

"Oh, I know I am," she frowned. "But I just felt so bad about what happened. I was just hoping to apologize to you again."

"Fine," he said dismissively, his aggravation clear in the way he narrowed his eyes. "Now please, just leave me alone."

"Do you think maybe..." Bekki scrunched up her nose and tilted her head slightly to the side. "I just feel like you don't believe me, I'd just really like to give you a hug," and before she finished she had her arms around him.

"Would you please!" Dan shouted with irritation. "Enough, are you crazy?" he demanded. Bekki slid her hand into his jacket pocket as she was releasing him, and retrieved his cell phone.

"I'm sorry, I just keep making things worse don't I?" she sighed sadly. "I honestly don't mean to."

"Just go," he demanded. "I don't want to hear about you bothering my wife either, understand?"

"Of course," Bekki nodded and apologized again. He shook his head and climbed into his car. As he drove off, Bekki held his cell phone in the palm of her hand. She made sure it was turned on. Then she walked back towards the bakery.

***

After several minutes had passed and Dan didn't return, Julie started to get suspicious. She tried calling his phone, but he didn't answer. She frowned as she checked the tracking app she had on her phone. She saw that he was headed for the bakery. If he had spoken to the police and then went to the bakery without telling her why, it could have something to do with the investigation. Julie couldn't take that chance.

She had to find out what he was up to. She grabbed her jacket and headed out of the motel, watching the blip on her phone the entire time.

Bekki paced back and forth inside the dark bakery. She had left the back door open, just as it had been on the night that Lydia died. She had Dan's cell phone on the counter. She knew it wouldn't be long before Julie came looking for him. In the few minutes she had, she did something that left her feeling very uncomfortable. She hung a noose from the rafter and let it dangle above a chair. In the shadows it was hard to see, but she knew it was there. Just the silhouette of it was enough to send shivers up and down her spine. She checked the voice recorder again to make sure it was still on. Within moments she heard the creak of the back door opening.

"Dan?" Julie called out as she walked into the front of the bakery. She flipped on the light switch and gasped as the noose was revealed to her in the stark fluorescent light.

"Dan's not here," Bekki said calmly as she met Julie's eyes. The woman had gone so pale that it was obvious she was shocked.

"What is this?" Julie demanded. "Why have you done this? Are you sick?"

Bekki folded her arms across her stomach and studied the woman intently.

"What I found that night was much more gruesome than this," Bekki said quietly. "To everyone who saw it, it looked as if a woman had taken her own life."

"That's because she did," Julie said with exasperation.

"Except, she didn't do it alone. She had help, didn't she Julie?" Bekki laid the back to an earring down on the counter. It looked almost exactly like the one she had seen on the floor. "I think we both know the truth. Don't we Julie?"

Julie held her breath for a moment as she stared at the back to the earring. She reached up and lightly touched her earlobe.

"I don't know what you're talking about," Julie insisted.

"You know, that knock to the back of my head was a hard one. Made me think you must have some experience with knocking people out. Do you Julie? Have you attacked someone in their home before?"

"You're insane," Julie stated angrily as she stalked around the side of the counter. "I could have you arrested for this!"

"You could," Bekki said slowly. "But you see, there's something that only Lydia and I knew."

"What?" Julie asked, too intrigued to ignore the bait.

"See people around here are very trusting. We don't lock our doors, we don't put in security cameras. But Lydia wasn't from here. She was from Chicago, like you," Bekki said. "She knew that danger could be around every corner. So she installed a camera. She didn't want to spook her customers, so she made sure it was concealed. The police didn't even find it when they searched the bakery."

"There's no camera," Julie said sternly. "Dan would know if there was a camera."

"Oh, there's a camera," Bekki insisted. "I helped her install it. I didn't think it was a big deal, since Lydia's death was just a suicide. I didn't want to hurt Dan more by telling him there was a video tape of it. But when I found the notepad, and then someone knocked me out and stole it, I decided it was time to take a look at that video tape. I wanted to see what really happened to Lydia."

Julie looked a whole lot less confident as she looked all around the room for the camera. "Where's the tape?" she demanded. "What have you done with it?"

"I saw some very interesting things on that tape," Bekki explained quietly.

"You didn't see anything!" Julie hissed. "Because there was nothing to see."

"Really?" Bekki asked. "It would have been the perfect crime. I doubt you even put your hands on Lydia, did you? No physical evidence to tie you to her murder. But, you didn't know about the camera."

"There is no camera!" Julie shouted, her voice nearing a shriek.

"If there's no camera then how do I know that you coaxed Lydia up on to that chair? How do I know that you watched as she put that noose around her own neck?"

Julie fell silent, her eyes wide, her lips forming words but offering no sound.

"That's right Julie," Bekki pressed. "I saw it all. I saw what you did to your own mother-in-law, your own family."

"She was never my family!" Julie spat out. Bekki felt the shift and knew that she had hit the right button.

"No? Did she try to break you and Dan up? Is that what happened?" Bekki asked in a more friendly tone. "I know moms are like that, always getting into their kids' business, instead of letting them live their lives."

"She did, she was always sticking her nose into things," Julie sighed and rubbed her forehead briefly.

"So, of course, you had to get rid of her," Bekki prompted, her eyes locked on Julie, her tone mild and not judging.

"Damn right I did," Julie spat out with more twang to her voice than Bekki had heard before. She certainly didn't sound like she was from Chicago. "I clawed my way up out of a dirt poor neighborhood in Georgia. Do you know how hard that is to do?" she demanded. "No, I don't imagine you would."

Bekki's eyes widened as she took a slight step back.

"You must have had to work hard."

"Work?" Julie laughed and shook her head. "I had to make myself into an entirely different person. I became Julie Ann, I became exactly what a man like Dan Brentwood would want. I placed myself right in his way, to make sure that he would notice me. When he did, I knew that was it, he was going to belong to me and I was going to spend the rest of my life with more money than I could ever spend."

Bekki's heartbeat quickened as the intense scowl on the woman's face only grew darker. "It was all going just fine, until that woman stuck her nose into our business. She started whispering things in Dan's ear, about making sure that I was who I said I was, about finding out about my family and my history," she shook her head and sneered. "She held on to her son so tightly that there was never any room for me. Then the wench had me tailed. She got pictures of me with a lover, and turned them over to her son. That was it. He immediately wanted a divorce, and I was going to lose everything."

Bekki frowned as she studied the woman in front of her. It was hard for her to fathom how anyone could believe that living that way was going to end up making them happy.

"Of course you were angry," Bekki prompted her. "You wanted to teach her a lesson."

"Sure I was angry," Julie smirked. "But I'm not stupid. I wasn't going to let her win. I knew if Dan lost his mother, he'd turn to me for comfort. He'd need me again. I knew he would forgive me if she wasn't there whispering in his ear."

Bekki felt her stomach churn as she recalled the way that Julie had positioned herself perfectly to comfort Dan after his mother's death.

"But you couldn't just kill her," Bekki said quietly, as if she understood completely. "It needed to be more tragic than that."

"Exactly," Julie nodded with a subtle smile of pride. "Like I said, I'm not stupid. So I convinced her that I had Dan locked up, that he was going to die, if she didn't do what I told her to do. She was so broken up about it, as if her precious little boy was the most important person in the world. So I gave her an ultimatum, either she kill herself or I'll shoot her and make her suffer a long death. I knew she would choose to kill herself because her brother had been shot years ago and she watched him die slowly. She would want to be in control and die quickly. She even put the noose around her own neck."

The rage that rose inside Bekki was so intense that she nearly lost her temper. She knew that if she showed any horror Julie might stop talking. She needed the full confession. She needed the truth to make sure that Julie would not find her way out of this.

"Brilliant," Bekki murmured, though she wanted to choke on the word. "Well you didn't even really kill her did you Julie? You just let her kill herself. Did you just stand there and watch? I mean, were you too scared to get your hands dirty?"

"I was going to," Julie admitted. "I was going to make her kick the chair out and everything, but I just couldn't. I wanted her to watch me do it. I wanted her to know that it was me that put an end to her meddling. So I kicked that chair out from under her," she laughed a little and shook her head. "You should have seen her face, she was so surprised."

Bekki's hands clenched at her sides. The woman had paid the ultimate price for the love of her son, and it was not something to laugh about.

"And now Dan's ready to reconcile, right?" Bekki asked in a trembling voice as she tried to swallow back her disgust.

"He tore up the divorce papers this afternoon," Julie said proudly. "Soon I'll be right back where I belong."

"Until he does something you don't like?" Bekki pointed out. "Is he expendable too?"

"Everyone's expendable, Bekki," the woman sighed. "I thought maybe you understood that."

Bekki faked a smile and stepped closer to the woman. When she spoke, she did in a low tone.

"I just wonder what Dan is going to think when he finds out that you killed his mother? Do you think he'll still want to reconcile?"

Julie laughed effortlessly, that same disdainful

laugh that Bekki heard from her before.

"Oh, he won't find out sweetheart. Did you really think you were walking out of this alive?"

Bekki felt her body tense as she recognized the flash of a gun at Julie's side. She hadn't been expecting that. Julie hadn't killed Lydia with a gun, so it hadn't crossed Bekki's mind that she would be carrying one.

"No one's going to believe I killed myself," Bekki warned, her eyes narrowed sharply. "If you hurt me, you'll be exposing yourself as a killer."

Julie laughed again and waved the gun in the air.

"Don't worry about that, they're not going to find your body. You'll leave a note, claiming you were so embarrassed by the false accusations that you made against me that you decided to go back to the city and leave Harroway behind once and for all. Sure, some people will wonder, but it isn't like you didn't disappear from this place once before," she smirked and began to raise the gun.

Bekki's entire body began to move instinctively. She did not take her eyes off Julie and could sense by the woman's slightest gesture which direction she was moving, and what her intentions were. When Bekki sprang into action, Julie was caught off guard by the flourish of movement. Bekki's hand struck the wrist that was holding the gun and bent it backward, causing Julie's fingers to unclench. The gun clattered to the floor. But Julie fought back, and nearly knocked Bekki off balance. The two had just tumbled to the floor and had begun grappling when Nick burst through the front door of the bakery. He had his gun drawn and aimed it directly at Julie. From the moment he met Bekki's eyes through the glass door of the bakery earlier in the evening, he had known she was up to something. He had been watching from outside the entire time.

"Put your hands up now!" he demanded. Julie ignored him and continued to claw at Bekki. Bekki managed to get her hands around the woman's flailing arms and pin them down on either side of her, while straddling her body. Nick kicked the fallen weapon out of the way and crouched down beside Julie. He had her cuffed in a matter of seconds.

"You can't do this!" Julie protested. "You don't have any proof of anything! I'll be out in an hour!"

Nick glanced up at Bekki who reached into her pocket and pushed the button on the tape recorder to play back their conversation.

Julie's face drained of all color as Nick helped her to her feet.

"I think you took care of the proof for us," he said calmly, his voice wavering only slightly with the disgust he felt for her actions. Bekki met the woman's eyes as she stood in front of her.

"Lydia was never someone who would take her life, Julie. You murdered a woman who was so loving she was willing to give up her own life to protect her son. You took her from the world, and now you're going to pay for it. Maybe heading back to Georgia would have been better than where you're going now."

Julie gasped as tears began flowing. They were not tears of grief, but tears of rage because she had not been able to get away with her master plan. As Nick led her out of the bakery, Bekki remained in the empty space. She knew that nothing she did would bring Lydia back, but at least now the rumors could be stamped out by the truth of what a brave and strong woman Lydia really was.

When Nick returned from handing Julie over to another officer to take her in for booking, he found Bekki still staring at the last place she had seen Lydia.

"Hey," he murmured softly from behind her as his warm hands rubbed at the curves of her shoulders. "It's over now," his gentle voice sought to soothe her.

"What if she hadn't left the door unlocked for me, Nick?" Bekki said quietly as she continued to stare. "What if Julie hadn't been able to get inside? What if I had showed up just a little earlier?"

"Bekki," he slid his arms around her shoulders and pulled her back against him. "You can't think that way. There are a million what ifs. What if you gave up and stopped investigating when I asked you to?"

Bekki turned to look up at him with surprise at his words. "What do you mean?" she asked.

"I mean, what if you didn't fight this hard for someone who you barely knew?" he asked in a whisper. "I don't know how you do it Bekki, how you see the truth so clearly."

"I wish I did," she replied hesitantly.

"You do," he insisted as he brushed her hair back from her eyes. "I look at a situation and I see the evidence, the proof, but you see more than that."

"I don't know about that," Bekki frowned as she glanced away from him.

"If it wasn't for you Bekki, Julie would have been free. She would have woven her spell over Dan again, at least until she decided he didn't need to be around any longer," he paused, took a short breath and then shook his head slowly. "I'm so amazed by you."

"Even my criminal activity?" she asked with an arched brow.

"Oh that," his expression grew a little more serious as he held her closer to him. "That's something we'll have to discuss."

"I swear I'm innocent," she grinned and he

kissed her lightly on the lips.

"Now that I don't believe for a second," he murmured just beside her ear. As they walked out of the bakery they found most of the town had come out to see what all the flashing lights were about. People gathered close as they watched Julie driven away in the back of a squad car. Sammy was among them. She walked over to Bekki and Nick, peering into the bakery curiously.

"Is everything okay?" she asked.

"I think it is now," Bekki said with a frown. "As okay as it can be."

***

Bekki was cleaning off the stations in the salon the next day when she heard the front door open. She didn't have any scheduled appointments. She turned to find Dan standing just inside the door.

"Hello," he said hesitantly.

"Hi Dan," Bekki said gently as she set down her spray and rag and walked towards him.

"I just wanted to thank you," he said quietly,

his face a sallow reflection of the pictures she had seen splashed all over the internet. "If it wasn't for you, I would have buried my mother never knowing the truth."

"I'm sorry Dan," Bekki said with a sigh. "I'm so sorry that this happened to you and to your mother."

"So am I," Dan agreed and stepped a little closer to her. "You know, I just never pictured a time when she wouldn't be here."

"She's still here," Bekki promised him. "I mean, everything she taught you, all the love she shared with you, none of that will ever truly be gone."

"You're right," he nodded solemnly but her words did not seem to give him much comfort. "I only wish I had paid more attention to her advice. She warned me about Julie, and I didn't listen. I thought I was in love."

"It's not your fault Dan," Bekki said firmly. "She was manipulating you from the start. You were her target, and her victim."

Dan nodded a little and then managed a half-smile. "Well, I just want you to know that if you ever need anything, anything at all, feel free to contact me. Okay?"

Bekki nodded and smiled in return. "Thanks Dan."

As he was turning to leave, he paused and turned back. "Also, the cake for your friend is in the freezer, I found it after Mom died and put it there in case someone came to pick it up. I know that my mother would have hated to see anyone miss out on a birthday cake. Please give it to your friend, find something to celebrate in all of this. That's what she would have wanted."

"Okay, I will," Bekki smiled warmly as she watched him walk out of the salon. It struck her that it didn't matter how much fame or wealth someone had, it did not provide them with any protection from some of the perils of life.

***

Later that night, when Dan had already begun his journey home, and Julie was safely behind bars, Bekki sat on her front porch, gazing up at the stars. The poles of the porch were lined with balloons and streamers. A big happy birthday sign hung in the window. As she took a sip of her glass of wine she reflected on how strange the entire week had been. So much had happened in such a short amount of time, and she didn't want Sammy to think that her birthday was forgotten.

"Hi there," Sammy called out as she walked up the driveway. "Is all of this for me?" she smiled.

"Yes," Bekki stood up to greet her friend and offered her a warm hug. "I'm sorry I've missed so many birthdays Sammy."

"It's okay Bekki," Sammy smiled at her. "I always admired you for getting out of this place and joining the real world. Didn't you know that?"

"No I didn't," Bekki laughed. "But I can tell you this. Now that I'm back, I wouldn't trade Harroway for a million cities."

"We wouldn't trade you either," Sammy winked lightly.

"Cake!" a shout came from the end of the driveway where Nick had parked his car. He was balancing a large sheet cake in his hands and not looking very confident about it.

"Wow!" Sammy gasped. "That has to be the

biggest cake I have ever seen!"

"It was supposed to be a big party," Bekki laughed. "But I bet we can handle it."

She hurried over to Nick to help him steady the cake on his way up the steps. Once they were all inside Nick laid the cake down on the dining room table.

"It's still a little frozen," he explained as he opened the lid.

"Not too frozen to taste the frosting I see," Bekki grinned when she noticed a finger mark in the creamy frosting.

"Oh uh," Nick blushed a little and then reached up to wipe at his mouth with a guilty expression.

"Tsk, tsk," Bekki laughed and grabbed a knife and some plates. As Bekki sliced into the cake Sammy smiled over her shoulder.

"It looks delicious, I only wish she was here to share it with us."

"In a way, maybe she is," Bekki said with a small smile as she served Sammy the first slice.

"At least now everyone knows the truth," Nick said as he slung an arm across Bekki's shoulders. "Thanks to the best detective without a badge."

"I don't need a badge, I can always borrow yours," she smiled up at Nick. He leaned down and kissed her gently.

"Look at the two of you, just like a blast from the past," Sammy laughed, her eyes wide and shining.

"No," Nick said firmly as he held Bekki close. "This isn't the past. This is the future."

As the three friends shared their cake, and the small town of Harroway once more fell into an assumption of safety, Bekki felt as if things were finally falling into place. Maybe it was time to let go of the hurt that Trevor had caused her with his betrayal. Maybe it was time to begin trusting again.

The End

More Cozy Mysteries by Cindy Bell

Heavenly Highland Inn Cozy Mystery Series

Murdering the Roses

Dead in the Daisies

Bekki the Beautician Cozy Mystery Series

Hairspray and Homicide

Mascara and Murder

Pageant and Poison

Conditioner and a Corpse

CPSIA information can be obtained
at www.ICGtesting.com
Printed in the USA
LVHW081142200422
716723LV00016BA/154